13155

*Return
to the
Lost Planet*

Return
to the
LOST PLANET

ANGUS MacVICAR

BURKE ★ *LONDON*

First published *1954*
Reprinted October *1954*

To
KEVIN SHELDON

Deus ex machina

Published by
Burke Publishing Co. Ltd.,
55 Britton Street, London E.C.1.
Printed in England by
C. Tinling & Co. Ltd.,
Liverpool, London & Prescot

CONTENTS

CHAPTER I

A Message from Space

FIVE DAYS.
They would be back in five days, bringing
Uncle Lachlan. That was what Spike and Hermanoff
had promised before taking off in the Professor's
ship. That was what the newspapers said, when, on
the day following their departure, the story was
published.

The black headlines of the *Daily Courier* streamed
across the page:—

McKINNON STILL ALIVE ON HESIKOS

DRAMATIC RESCUE BID

Yesterday afternoon, shattering the moorland
peace of Inverard, in North Argyll, atomically
powered jets burst into action. For the second
time in two months a space ship took off for the
"lost planet," its fiery trail vanishing wisp-like
into the blue autumn sky.

Inside were the European scientist, Professor
Hermanoff, and Spike Stranahan, the young
American engineer. They were speeding to the
rescue of the leader of the last expedition, Dr.
Lachlan McKinnon, alone and in grave danger
among the icy wastes of Hesikos.

7

Other members of the first successful space expedition remained at Inverard — Jeremy Grant, Dr. McKinnon's seventeen-year-old nephew; Professor Lars Bergman, his Swedish partner; Janet Campbell, his pretty nineteen-year-old secretary; and Madge Smith, the grey-haired, sharp-tongued Cockney cook.

In five days' time they expect the ship to return. . . .

To me those days seemed very long.

Professor Bergman was busy with his papers, arranging material for the scientific book he intended to publish on our voyage to Hesikos. Janet was busy, too, making notes and typing from his dictation. Madge had to cook, not only for us, but also for Jock Ferguson, and the workmen; while in her spare time, convinced that during our absence the house had been neglected, she darted about in a frenzy of spring-cleaning. None of them, therefore, had much time to worry.

But like Jock Ferguson and his men, I hadn't a great deal to do. After an hour's maintenance work in the testing-sheds each morning, I found myself at a loose end; and as time went on anxiety began to nag at me.

Inverard was at its loveliest. From the front door of the massive, turreted house, I could see the green glen and the burn which ran through it with a lulling tinkle. Beyond the glen were the tall firs surrounding the launching-platform, and beyond the firs swathes of purple moorland stretching far into the distance.

The sun was warm and pleasant. In any other circumstances I should have been happy and content. But the days were passing, and though each night Janet and I kept listening watch by the light-wave radio receiver in the library, no message came through from Hermanoff and Spike.

Again and again, like scenes in a film, the events of the past two months scurried through my head.

My journey from Australia, after the death of my parents there. The startling discovery that Uncle Lachlan and Professor Bergman, assisted by Spike Stranahan, were building an atomically powered space ship, in which they proposed to travel three hundred thousand miles to Hesikos, the "lost planet" referred to by Plato.

The visit of Hermanoff, the bitter-tongued scientist who was building another space ship in Europe, with the intention of reaching Hesikos before Uncle Lachlan.

The journey to Hesikos, so filled with excitement that my recollection of it had the nebulous quality of a dream. The crash-landing. The lovely pastel colours of Hesikos. Rocky Valley and the creeping mist. Finally, there had been our meeting with Hermanoff and his assistant Andrieff. . . .

I could always remember that meeting with extraordinary vividness. Hermanoff and Andrieff had landed on Hesikos only a few days behind us. Our ship had been damaged beyond hope of repair, and we expected them to reject our plea for assistance. But Hesikos had brought about a change in Hermanoff. When winter threatened, its lethal fingers of ice covering the flowers and the green moss, he had become our friend and brought all of us back to Earth.

All of us, that is, except Uncle Lachlan. He had stayed behind, so that there might be no danger of overcrowding in Hermanoff's small ship.

At first it had seemed certain that he would die in the terrible cold. But one night soon after our return, when Janet and I were listening-in to the radio, a message had come to us in Morse. It was from Uncle Lachlan. He had reached the shelter of his own ship in time and was telling us that he was still alive.

Next day, realising that the batteries in Uncle Lachlan's ship would only last a short time and that he was depending on them for sufficient warmth to keep him alive, Professor Hermanoff had decided to go back to Hesikos in an attempt at rescue. Spike had gone, too, in charge of the motor and the jets.

And now we were waiting—waiting for their return in five days. . . .

One morning I was sitting on the front door step, thinking, when suddenly there was a sound behind me. I looked up to see Professor Bergman standing in the doorway, his bulging waistcoat sprinkled with tobacco ash, his stout face sombre and sympathetic.

"There is no need to have anxiety, Jeremy. Not yet. They have been gone only three days."

I knew he was talking sense, but the germ of uneasiness kept attacking my nerves. "Janet and I have been listening every night," I said. "There hasn't been a sound."

He shrugged. "Conditions may have been against good reception. Hermanoff's transmitter may be temporarily out of order." Patting my shoulder he went on: "Come, Jeremy, Madge tells me lunch is ready. There is your favourite apple-tart. . . ."

Another day passed—and another. Five days, and still no news.

I tried to control my fears. I told myself again and again that the timetable worked out by Hermanoff and Spike had been too rigid, allowing for no errors or delays. Sixty hours to reach Hesikos. Fifty-four and a half hours coming back. That left only six hours to make contact with Uncle Lachlan on Hesikos. Perhaps Hermanoff and Spike had landed farther away from Uncle Lachlan's ship than they had intended.

Another day. Another night listening by the radio. I knew that even Janet and Madge were becoming nervous, though they tried not to show it.

In the morning I went to see Professor Bergman in the study. "It's almost a week now. Do you think anything has happened?"

He put down his pen and began to polish his glasses. "We cannot tell, Jeremy. I myself am not inclined to be pessimistic. Hermanoff, Spike and Dr. McKinnon are all men of courage and resource."

"But they promised to send a message."

"As I said before, it is possible that their transmitter has broken down. Next thing we know Hermanoff's ship may be landing on the moor, as happened after our first journey to Hesikos."

I detected a lack of conviction in his voice. "All

day today," I said, "I've had a feeling—as if something had gone wrong."

He smiled. "It is your imagination. You must try to be patient——"

"I *have* been patient!" I blurted out. "I haven't said a word. But—I can't stand it much longer."

"I know how you feel. Believe me, my boy. . . . But there is nothing we can do, except wait."

That night Janet and I again kept listening watch. As we sat there in the library, with the clock ticking on towards morning, we could hear a thin wind whining through the trees outside and sometimes, in the distance, the eerie hoot of an owl. But the radio remained silent, except for an occasional faint crackle of atmospherics, like dry leaves burning. Shortly after five o'clock Janet made a cup of tea; but it didn't do us much good. We grew colder and even more miserable.

At six o'clock I got up and fiddled with the dials for about the hundredth time. There was a whistle and some oscillation, but nothing else. Light from outside was beginning to show behind the drawn curtains.

I glanced at Janet. As if reading my thoughts she said: "Not much chance any more tonight. Spike told us it would be no good listening in daylight."

"What d'you think has gone wrong?"

"I don't know. If only we *knew*. . . ."

"I'm trying to believe their transmitter has been damaged," I said.

The door opened. Madge stood there in curlers and a padded dressing-gown. As she came towards us, her thin face was puckered in concern.

"You two still 'ere? I 'eard you talking and came to ask if you'd like some 'ot coffee."

Janet shook her head. "Thank you, Madge, but we've had a cup of tea. We're just going to bed."

"Pore souls—you look real tired. You 'eard nothing, I suppose?"

"Not a thing." Janet pressed her hands together. "Oh, Madge—it's almost more than I can bear!"

"I know, ducks. I wish I could 'elp. . . . Never mind, better luck tomorrow——"

She broke off. We looked at one another in quick astonishment. And as we waited, distrusting the evidence of our ears, we heard it again—a faint stutter from the radio.

My mouth grew dry and salty. I stood there like a fool, holding my breath, until at last Janet roused me to action.

"Quick, Jeremy! Turn up the volume!"

I knelt down and adjusted the control, and the chattering Morse burst out almost in my face.

Madge came and stood immediately behind me, gripping my shoulder. "Blimey—is it from *them?*" she whispered.

"Wait, Madge!" As usual Janet was practical. She snatched up a pencil and pad from the table and began to copy down the dots and dashes. After a moment she said: "Yes. PH—Planet Hesikos. It's their identification signal!"

I felt myself trembling. The pent-up anxiety of the past week drained away, leaving me weak and almost incapable of coherent thought.

Then I heard Janet's voice as she translated. "PH

calling Inverard. PH calling Inverard. Message from Hermanoff and Stranahan. . . ."

The moment of reaction passed. I began to feel strong and confident again.

Madge bent down and kissed my cheek.

CHAPTER II

Night Journey

FIVE MINUTES later I burst into Professor Berg-man's room. He sat up in bed, blinking as I switched on the table-lamp.

"It's come," I exclaimed. "There's been a message. Janet and I heard it—and Madge, too."

"From Hermanoff and Spike?"

"Yes. Their transmitter *was* damaged. But they've repaired it. And—and Uncle Lachlan's safe."

His round, sleepy face broke into a smile as he caught my arm. "My boy, I am so glad. I tried to hide it, but really I had begun to be anxious."

"They found him alive and well," I hurried on, "and brought him to Hermanoff's ship, using the space suits."

"It is wonderful news! And now they are coming back to Earth?"

My excitement waned a little. "No," I said. "That's the trouble. They *can't* come back."

His eyes widened. "They cannot come back? What do you mean?"

"The message explained it. Not only the trans-mitter but the whole ship was damaged—by the intense cold. The hull is cracked, just above the jets, and they're afraid it would break up altogether if they tried to take off."

"I see. Violent contraction of the metal was a danger we had foreseen. But the effect must have been more serious than we thought."

I continued: "They say they're quite safe for the present. They have a number of spare batteries, and the heaters in Professor Hermanoff's ship are keeping out the cold."

"We must be thankful for that," he said, then added thoughtfully: "They also have plenty of food—enough to last for four months, I believe. By that time winter in the northern part of Hesikos should be over."

"But—but their ship's damaged," I reminded him. "How are they going to get back?"

He got up, put on a dressing-gown and began to collect his shaving-tackle. "That is *our* problem," he answered. "Fortunately we have time to consider ways and means. Four months at least."

But though I went to bed and slept until seven in the evening, the thought of my uncle and the others remained at the back of my mind. I dreamt about them—alone on Hesikos, huddled around the heaters in Hermanoff's ship, with only a thin steel wall between them and the freezing white layers of ice and snow outside; three lonely men in a world of deadly cold. They were alive and had enough to eat, but I knew that already they must be longing to talk to us again, to taste one of Madge's famous apple-tarts, or even to hear the birds and smell the perfume of the firs at Inverard.

After supper that night we had a conference in the library—Janet and Madge, Professor Bergman and myself.

Madge said: "Wot I'd like to know is—can they repair their ship when the warm weather comes?"

Slowly Bergman shook his head. "They would need a welding plant, like the one in our workshop. Not only that—if the hull is cracked there must be a certain amount of warping, which is bound to get worse as the winter cold continues."

"Would there be any chance of transferring the atomic motor from Professor Hermanoff's ship to Dr. McKinnon's?" Janet asked.

"I am afraid not. It is the wrong size. And a different design."

I said that in my opinion there was only one answer to the problem. "We must build another ship here, then go and bring them back. It's what Uncle Lachlan would do in our place."

Janet looked doubtful, but Madge supported me at once. "You're right, son, and as long as you're alive your Uncle Lachlan will be alive, too—stubborn and determined as they come!"

"But the expense!" exclaimed Janet. "A new ship would cost a fortune."

"Uncle Lachlan has a good deal of money left," I pointed out. "His lawyer told me so, just the other day."

Professor Bergman's broad chin rested in both his hands. After a time he said: "I agree with Jeremy. We must have another ship. And I myself can give assistance, financially. But what makes me worry is something else. Without Spike, our engineer, how can we design and build it? I have a theoretical knowledge of the various instruments. But to erect the hull—to manufacture the instruments them-

B

selves—well, I am ignorant of the practical side."

"Surely we can find another engineer," said Janet. "In America, perhaps."

"I do not think so. It is highly specialised work."

An idea occurred to me. "What about Hermanoff's assistant—Andrieff? He would help us. He built Hermanoff's ship."

"But 'asn't 'e gone back to 'is own country?" Madge put in.

Janet leaned forward. For the first time excitement and enthusiasm sparkled in her eyes. "Not yet," she answered. "I noticed he gave an interview to a newspaper, the day before yesterday. He's in London. But flying home quite soon, I think."

"Then we must catch him before he goes," I said. "Once he leaves this country we may never find him again."

"Where is 'e staying in London?" asked Madge. "Did it say, love?"

"It didn't, actually. But the paper ought to know." Janet got quickly to her feet. "The *Daily Courier* it was. I'll ring them up right away."

Bergman nodded. "It is the best plan."

I went with Janet to the telephone and heard her call being put through to the News Editor. He remembered at once the interview with Andrieff and within a few moments was able to quote from a file on his desk.

"He's been staying at the Caird Hotel. But he left London this morning, and I'm afraid you'll have to hurry if you want to contact him. He's flying to Europe tonight—from Renfrew Airport."

"Tonight!"

"Yes. So I understand."

"Oh, dear!" Janet was taken aback. "Can you say when his plane is due to leave?"

"Sorry. I'm not a magician." The voice over the telephone was inclined to be dry. "But you could find out from the Airport, I suppose."

"Yes. Yes, of course. Thank you so much."

A clerk at Renfrew supplied the information. "Berlin, madam? There is a plane to Berlin at midnight. A direct flight—no calls. But if you wish to make a reservation, I'm afraid——"

"That's all right," Janet interrupted. "I just wanted to make sure of the time."

"I see." The clerk paused for a moment, then added: "The bus leaves St. Enoch Station in Glasgow at eleven-thirty."

"Oh, thank you."

At Inverard, however, we were a hundred miles from Glasgow, and it was now nearly eight o'clock. At first we considered calling Renfrew again—just before midnight—with a request that Andrieff should be found and brought to the telephone to speak to us. Then we realised that his English was so bad that he might not understand what we were trying to say. In any case, if he were interrupted in a last minute chaos of ticket and passport checking, he would be unlikely to listen calmly to our proposals.

Finally I said: "Why should we worry about 'phoning? If Janet and I started off now—in the jeep—we could be at St. Enoch Station about eleven. That would give us time to talk to Andrieff before he left in the bus."

Both Madge and Professor Bergman thought it was

a good idea. But Janet looked thoughtful. "We'd have to drive pretty fast," she said. "And some of the roads are awful."

Bergman patted her shoulder. "It is the best way —and you can do it, my dear. The crux of the matter is this. If Andrieff does not help us, then I am afraid we cannot build a ship ourselves—in four months."

Ten minutes later, having checked the petrol, oil and water, I climbed into the jeep beside Janet. With Madge and the Professor waving from the front door, we drove away on the narrow moorland track which joined the main Glasgow road at Dalmally.

The first part of the journey was comparatively easy. There was little traffic, and though the road surface was uneven, the well-sprung jeep travelled on briskly at over thirty miles per hour. The sun, sinking towards the peaked mountains of the west, remained at our backs, and its glare, therefore, caused us no annoyance. We passed through Dalmally and reached Crianlarich shortly after nine o'clock.

Then things became more difficult. The sun went down and Janet had to drive in a confusing twilight. The road twisted and turned along the banks of Loch Lomond, with shadowy trees on one side and slate-grey water on the other. Right-angled corners took us by surprise. Sheep and long-horned Highland cattle wandered out in front of us, like ghosts in the gloaming. By the time we got to Tarbet we were beginning to fall behind schedule.

In spite of her dainty appearance, however, Janet was a good driver. When darkness settled down and the headlights became really useful, she put her foot hard on the accelerator and gradually regained lost time.

Once the headlights flickered and almost went out, and it suddenly occurred to me that Jock Ferguson had said something about a loose connection. But they came on again strongly, and I kept my fingers crossed.

As we swung past Inverbeg I glanced at my wrist watch. It was just after ten o'clock, and according to the speedometer we still had thirty miles to go. Tension began to creep into my muscles, but I said nothing to Janet.

The jeep was open, and her thick dark hair fluttered like a flag. I asked if she was cold, but she shook her head and drove even faster. Though I was wearing two jerseys and a lumber-jacket, I had begun to shiver myself.

Then we swooped down a long hill and came out of the darkness into Balloch and Alexandria. In a way it was comforting to think that we should now have the benefit of street lamps all the way to Glasgow.

Beyond Alexandria, with the firefly lights of Dumbarton on our right, Janet eased her position at the wheel and said: "Seventeen more miles, Jeremy. What's the time?"

"Quarter to eleven."

She nodded. "We'll make it, I think."

But I wasn't so sure. Such a lot depended on the jeep. And in forty-five minutes Andrieff would be climbing into the bus at St. Enoch Station.

Then it happened. We were travelling slowly at a corner—which was lucky—when suddenly we heard a sharp explosion and felt an ominous bumping at the front. The jeep swerved a little, but Janet brought it under control almost at once and pulled up near the kerb.

It was a puncture all right. For a moment I felt sick with disappointment. But Janet's brisk, determined voice brought me to my senses.

"Thank goodness there's a spare wheel at the back! Come on, Jeremy—I'll get it out, if you jack up the front."

We kept the headlights on. I dived for the jack, thrust it below the front axle and had the flat tyre clear of the ground in a matter of seconds. Janet dumped the spare wheel on the road beside me and found a spanner. The nuts were stiff, but I kicked hard on the spanner and soon had them off. Then between us we fitted on the spare. As I screwed the nuts on again Janet began to lower the jack.

When we had finished I looked at my watch and found that the whole operation had taken less than five minutes.

"We'll do it yet," said Janet, letting in the clutch. But on the outskirts of Glasgow we were held up for another five minutes by an opening bridge. As we sped down Buchanan Street towards St. Enoch Station it was twenty minutes past eleven, and to make matters worse the lights were against us at Argyll Street. I felt suddenly desperate. With only another five hundred yards to go, it would be the irony of fate if we missed Andrieff after all.

At last, however, the green lights came on and we were able to cross the tramlines and turn into St. Enoch Square. As we pulled up near the Airport

Office it was twenty-seven minutes past eleven. We scrambled out and saw to our relief that an empty bus was standing at the entrance.

A line of passengers appeared and began to get into it. Among them was Andrieff.

CHAPTER III

The Power from Hesikos

H E WAS stoutly built, with the broad smooth face of a Slav. As we ran to meet him he suddenly smiled and held out his hands.

"Why, it is Janet—and Jeremy! I am so happy to see you. But why——"

Janet pulled him out of the line of passengers. "We've come from Inverard," she told him. "We need you—to help us build a new ship."

"A new ship?" All at once he loooked nervous and ill-at-ease. "But that is impossible. I am going back to my own country to build one for my Government. I have been offered fifty thousand pounds."

It seemed that the frustrations of our journey were not yet over. "We—we can't offer you that," I said. "On the other hand——"

The engine of the bus started up. The conductor said loudly: "Half-past eleven. All aboard, please."

Andrieff turned away from us. "I am sorry, my friends, I have to go. If you had approached me sooner—yesterday, perhaps——"

"Oh, but you *mustn't* go!" Janet clung to his arm. "You've *got* to help us. It's about Dr. McKinnon, and Spike, and Professor Hermanoff. Haven't you seen the papers?"

He shook his head. "I cannot read the English papers."

"All aboard," repeated the conductor, firmly. "Come now, miss, the driver is waiting."

She appealed to him. "Can't we get in the bus and go to the Airport with our friend?"

"Certainly, miss. The return fare is five shillings."

I thought that was the end, for I had come away without a penny in my pockets. By some miracle, however, Janet found a ten shilling note in her purse. Having got our tickets, we climbed into the bus and sat beside Andrieff in the back seat.

"But I assure you," he said, spreading his hands, "there is no good coming with me. I have promised my government. The contract is signed."

The bus moved away. "Anyway, please listen to what we have to tell you," said Janet. "If you haven't read the papers you can't possibly understand."

"Very well. But I must insist—I have to return to my country tonight. The matter is one of urgency."

As the bus bumped and swung across Jamaica Bridge, then turned sharp right into Paisley Road, she told him what had happened. Andrieff listened, his face impassive. I tried to discover signs of interest or sympathy in his expression, but there was none— not even when Janet described the dramatic message we had received from Hesikos.

Finally she said: "That's all we know, Andrieff. Dr. McKinnon and Spike and Professor Hermanoff are marooned on the planet, with enough food for only four months."

"I see," he answered.

"We must try to rescue them," she hurried on.

"And for that we need another space ship. As far as we know, you're the only engineer who could build one—besides Spike, that is. If you won't help us, it'll mean they can never get back to Earth."

And now I saw a look of real distress in his eyes. "Surely there is someone else," he began.

She cut in, sharply. "There may be someone else. We know that, Andrieff. Or someone could learn. But the point is, you have the experience. No one else could *learn* to build a space ship in four months. And we've got to reach Hesikos in four months, before their food comes to an end."

He looked down at his thick-soled shoes. At last he said: "I understand. I understand the position now."

"Then you will help us?" I asked.

For a long time he didn't answer. His strong, curiously slim hands remained clasped together on his knees. Then, like some uneasy animal in a cage, he moved his head from side to side. "I have told you, it is impossible. While I am in London, waiting for transport to take me home, a person from our Embassy came to my hotel. He said to me—'Andrieff, you have brought glory to our country. You will bring more. You will build a space ship for our Government—a ship to carry many passengers and technical instruments. If you do that we will pay you fifty thousand pounds and make you independent.' So I signed the contract yesterday, and I cannot break it now."

A small pulse of desperation had begun to beat in Janet's temple, but she kept her voice steady. "I know it is difficult," she agreed.

He nodded, his brown eyes seeing a distant vision. "I am a poor man once. My father was a peasant, labouring in the fields. In the War he died—of starvation. He became ill, and had no money, and so he starved. To be rich, to know that I can live always in comfort—that has been my ambition since my father died."

She touched his hands. "We understand that. We can also understand that you want to do your duty by your country. But——"

"I cannot break my word," he interrupted. "I tell you I cannot."

"You could telephone your Embassy," I suggested. "You could say you had to postpone the contract for six months."

"Jeremy, you do not understand!" he exclaimed, so loudly that some of the other passengers looked round in surprise. "If I did that I would be called a traitor —a saboteur. I would no longer remain a citizen of my own country. I would lose the fifty thousand pounds and all my dream of security. . . . No, it is impossible. I am sorry. . . ."

"But think, Andrieff!" The pulse in Janet's temple was beating quicker now. "If you don't help us it will mean that Dr. McKinnon, Spike and your friend Professor Hermanoff may die before we can get to them."

"I know! I know that! Do not say it!"

"You were with us on Hesikos," I reminded him, as a last resort. "One of the first men in the world to reach another planet. You can't let your old comrades down."

He refused to look me in the face. "They may

survive," he muttered. "You may reach them in time without my help."

The bus went on, through the dark streets to the Airport. In another few minutes we should be there. In another few minutes Andrieff would step into the plane for Berlin, and we should never see him again. I felt helpless and miserable, and I know Janet was the same. Three hundred thousand miles away, among the ice and snow of Hesikos, Uncle Lachlan and the others were waiting for help; and we had failed them.

And then, quite suddenly and unexpectedly, I felt renewed confidence.

I glanced at the others and saw that Andrieff was speaking quietly to himself: "What are riches? What are riches compared with the love of friends? Do riches bring peace?"

Suddenly he looked up with an expression on his face of utter incredulity. Our fellow passengers were sitting undisturbed, smoking, reading newspapers, leaning back with half-closed eyes.

Janet said: "We're almost at the Airport, Andrieff."

"I know," he answered, with quiet deliberation. "But I am afraid the 'plane must leave without me."

I caught his arm. "You mean you'll come back to Inverard and build a new ship for us?"

"Yes. I will go back. I will build your ship. Otherwise—even though I became rich and powerful in my own country—there would be no peace in my mind."

"Thank you," said Janet, in a whisper; and I noticed she had grown pale.

CHAPTER IV

An Exhausted Bird

WE DROVE Andrieff back to Inverard, reaching there about four o'clock in the morning, before the sun came up. We had 'phoned from Glasgow, while an all-night garage was repairing the punctured tyre, and Madge and Bergman were waiting for us with plenty of hot coffee.

Next day we began work on the new ship, Bergman drawing the plans and Andrieff translating them into terms of toughened steel.

As the weeks went by the huge red hull began to take shape behind the fir wood. The workmen—under my uncle's foreman, Jock Ferguson—moved like ants among the steel scaffolding. From dawn till dusk, and sometimes throughout the night, the sound of their drills and hammers was constantly in the background. But no one worried about the noise—we were all too busy, too intent upon our scheme of rescuing Uncle Lachlan and Spike and Hermanoff.

The autumn sun shone brightly, day after day; but in time the nights grew darker and a breath of winter chilled the atmosphere. The brilliant purple of the heather began to fade.

At first we received a message from Hesikos every five days, but as the batteries in Hermanoff's stranded

ship gradually lost power, we heard from Uncle
Lachlan and the others at longer and longer intervals. It seemed they remained well, however, and
were still able to defy the cold.

One night, towards the end of the fourteenth week,
we all gathered in the library to listen-in at the stated
time, for the previous message had warned us to
expect something of importance. The second-hand
of the stop-watch crept up to ten o'clock, and Janet
got her pencil and paper ready. For once even Madge
grew silent.

And then we had a considerable shock. Instead of
the usual crackle of Morse, a voice came from the
loudspeaker, faint and remote but nevertheless
distinct. "Planet Hesikos. Planet Hesikos calling
Inverard. . . ."

It was Uncle Lachlan. We looked at each other in
amazement, and Andrieff's face lost its impassivity.
Madge was about to speak, but Professor Bergman
held up his hand for silence.

"This is our last message, for the batteries are
almost done. But yesterday the ice and snow began
to melt, and we can now open the hatch and go
outside, without the space suits. Today we visited
the other ship, and Spike has used parts of the old
transmitter, so that this one can relay speech as well
as Morse. We look forward to your coming. We are
all in good health, but are growing tired of our own
company and a continual diet out of tins."

"Poor souls!" whispered Madge, with the ghost of a
smile for Uncle Lachlan's characteristically wry
humour. "Never a decent meal all these weeks."

"Ssh! He's not finished yet," Janet warned her.

"When you come," continued the voice, with its perceptible Scots burr, "bring the jeep. Two hours ago we saw a strange sign—a small, exhausted bird, perched on a rock outside. We must explore the central areas of Hesikos, and for that a jeep will be an advantage. We shall find life there—I am sure of it. The little bird is proof . . . Au revoir, my friends— we hope to see you soon. . . ."

That was all that came through, and presently I switched off. For some time none of us spoke. It was as if a miracle had happened. Our friends were still safe and had passed through the worst of the winter. And from a distance of three hundred thousand miles we had just heard Uncle Lachlan's own voice.

Then something else occurred to me. "Did you hear what he said?" I asked. "About the small bird?"

Bergman nodded. "I am not surprised."

"Do you mean there may be 'uman creatures on 'Esikos after all!" said Madge, her eyes widening.

"I do not know," he answered. "But there is evidence that in the central or equatorial belt the cold is never as severe as in the north, where we landed. And the fossils we found show that once upon a time there was abundant life."

"It's extraordinary," said Janet. "Dr. McKinnon would never have mentioned such a thing, if he hadn't been sure."

After a moment I said: "Andrieff, when will the new ship be ready?"

He glanced across at me and smiled. "The hull is complete—also the atomic motor. It now depends on the instruments."

"They have all been manufactured," replied Professor Bergman. "Only testing is now required."

"And will there be room for the jeep?" I asked him.

"Plenty of room. On the outward journey at least. Though with the other three on board we may not be able to bring it back."

"When can we go, then?"

He tapped the table with his stout sensitive fingers. "In my opinion, Jeremy, we can fly to Hesikos in one week from now."

That night I remained awake for a long time. In my mind's eye was a recurring picture—the picture of a little bird perched on a rock on faraway Hesikos. Its wings were bedraggled and tired, but the spark of life shone steadily in its small, bright eyes.

CHAPTER V

Zero Minus

DURING THAT last week our principal task was the tuning of the atomic motor. Bergman and Andrieff spent hours in the testing shed, running it in on the bench, and its eldritch scream echoed about the house a dozen times each day.

There was, it seemed, a certain amount of trouble with the timing. One of the bevel-gears was fractionally out of alignment, causing a roughness in starting. Andrieff worked on it, with patient thoroughness. Though at full speed the motor performed faultlessly, and Bergman would have passed it without further examination, he persisted in his policy of absolute perfection.

"When so much is at stake there is no room for error," he said. "This motor must run continuously for the sixty hours it will take you to reach Hesikos."

In the end, however, the timing was adjusted to his satisfaction. The motor was installed in the ship and connected to the bank of six enormous jets, which, when in action, would expel atomically charged droplets of water at the almost incredible speed of over seven miles per second.

We were due to take off for Hesikos on a Friday— Janet and Madge, Professor Bergman and myself— and the old superstition that to start a journey on a

Friday means bad luck never once occurred to us. On the Thursday afternoon the installation of the motor was complete, and Janet and I went down through the wood to see the workmen streamlining the junction between the jets and the main part of the hull.

We stood at the foot of the long steel ladder, looking up.

"They'll be finished in another hour or so," said Janet. "Then everything will be quiet until tomorrow at twelve. How do you feel about it, Jeremy?"

"Not bad. Better than last time."

"I wish Andrieff were coming with us."

"So do I. But I don't blame him for wanting to go back to his own country. They've forgiven him for coming to work with us, but if he went to Hesikos that would be the last straw. They'd probably decide he really was a saboteur."

She nodded. After a moment she said: "I suppose Professor Bergman will be able to handle the controls all right. Anyway, if something does go wrong—well, there's not much *anyone* can do in outer space!"

I thought she looked pinched and tired. "What's worrying you?" I asked. "You're not usually such an old sobersides."

"Sorry, Jeremy." She looked down at her red sandals. "The fact is, I have a feeling this journey isn't going to be as easy as our last."

"But why?" I exclaimed. "You haven't got second sight, have you?"

"Of course not." She tried to smile. "I expect it's just plain nerves—and knowing how much Dr.

McKinnon and Hermanoff and Spike are depending on us. And there's something else. I mean, leaving all this behind—the green firs, and the wind sighing through them, and the stream tinkling down there in the glen. And on Hesikos everything so quiet and still—no movement, no sound even."

"I know how you feel. But remember what Uncle Lachlan said in his message. He's sure people live there, farther south."

"Yes, I'd forgotten that. . . . Oh, don't pay any attention to me, Jeremy. Six weeks of hard work have left us all on edge. . . . Come on. We have a job to do—all those instruments to check."

She said nothing more about her premonition, and as we worked inside the ship, testing each instrument in turn, she was as efficient and capable as ever. From Professor Bergman, who came to examine the control panel in the main compartment, we learned that Madge had already put most of the food aboard, while Jock had loaded on the jeep and a number of sticks of gelignite which Uncle Lachlan needed for geological survey.

"Where's Andrieff?" I asked.

"In the testing-shed," Bergman replied. "I have done a calculation on the escape velocity—which has to be more than eleven point-one kilometres per second—and he is making sure that all the engineering figures are correct. . . . Now, if you will excuse me, there is a little fault in the main jet control which must be put right."

By seven o'clock that evening the work was done, and we could rest until twelve the following day. The radar-screens, the telescopes, the light-wave radio

and the navigational instruments were all in working
order. The main jets, which would lift us from the
Earth and propel us through space to Hesikos; the
rotatory jets, which would make the ship spin and
create artificial gravity and allow us to walk about
on the curved hull as if it were flat; the air-pressure
system and the parachute landing-gear in the
forward compartment—everything had been checked
and re-checked. But though we went to bed early, I
don't believe any of us slept very much. I kept
thinking of Uncle Lachlan and Spike and Hermanoff,
so far away on Hesikos, their lives depending on our
skill.

In the morning, however, most of our anxieties
were for ourselves—at least mine were. But when I
went down for breakfast Madge was just coming into
the dining-room with a fresh supply of ham and eggs,
and she, to my surprise, appeared quite happy and
carefree.

"Morning, son," she smiled, heaping my plate.
"Never start a journey on an empty stomach—that's
my motto."

"You're not scared," I asked.

"Well, I dunno." She stood by the sideboard, her
grey head on one side like a bird. "You never get
used to it, do you? Specially that awful take-off."

I nodded. "And this waiting makes it worse.
There's still three hours till mid-day."

"I'm not grumbling about that," she said. "And
me with all this washing-up to do. . . . 'Ere, take
another egg, son—it's a shame to waste them."

"What about the others?"

"Well, Professor Bergman and Mr. Andrieff 'ave

finished long ago, and I'm sure Janet won't be so very 'ungry when she comes down. 'Ere you are, Jeremy—it's done just as you like it, on both sides."

"Thank you, Madge."

"That's fine. There's plenty of toast, too."

I spread butter on another slice. "It's funny, in sixty-three hours from now we may be sitting down to another meal in Hesikos, with Uncle Lachlan."

She looked serious for a moment. "Yes, it makes you think," she admitted.

Presently Janet came in, and I could see that her feelings were more like mine. She refused ham and eggs and breakfasted on a cup of tea and a morsel of toast.

"How did you sleep?" she asked me.

"Not very well."

"Neither did I. I must have counted about a million sheep."

Madge patted her shoulder. "Well, ducks, it's only natural to be excited—specially at your age. Even Professor Bergman was a bit silent this morning, and 'e's no chicken." Rather more quietly she added: " 'E said to remind you—all aboard by 'alf-past eleven."

Janet took a final sip of tea. "Zero minus thirty. As if we'd forget!"

I asked Madge what she thought about her kitchen in the ship.

"Oh, it's lovely," she said with enthusiasm. "Once we take off the first thing I'll do is bake Dr. McKinnon's favourite cake. Remember—with the coffee-icing? Poor Dr. McKinnon—when 'e was in a good mood 'e used to say to me, 'That's why I picked you as my 'ousekeeper, Madge; on account of your coffee-cake!' "

Neither Janet nor I could help laughing, and as we gave a hand to clear away the breakfast things, I for one felt better.

At half-past eleven Andrieff accompanied Professor Bergman and me to the foot of the ship's ladder. His job was to wait there at the inter-com. until eleven fifty-five. Then it would be time for him to take cover in the cellars with Jock Ferguson and the other workmen.

Bergman shook his hand. "Janet and Madge have both gone aboard. So—good-bye, Andrieff."

"Good-bye, Professor Bergman."

"Jeremy and I shall always be grateful for what you have done."

"Gosh, yes," I put in. "It's a great ship, and we could never have built it without you."

His smooth cheeks were slightly pale, his lips more compressed than usual. "I am glad that I decided to help," he answered.

"Good-bye, then. And good luck—in your own country."

"Thank you." It seemed that he wanted to say more, but the words did not come. "Good-bye," he said, simply.

At eleven-fifty we closed the main hatch, shutting out the sky and the trees and the fresh autumn air. Inside the ship was a faint metallic odour, but the lighting and the air-pressure system appeared to be working well. Janet spoke to Andrieff through the inter-com., warning him to make sure there was nothing inflammable near the jets and saying a final good-bye.

Then Professor Bergman took charge. "Jeremy, will you take the controls?" As I moved to the panel he added: "And please—all fasten your safety-belts."

I glanced at the clock and saw that it was two minutes to twelve.

The Professor went on: "We have all experienced a take-off before, but may I remind you of the sequence of events? When I give the order Jeremy will start the atomic motor. In a few seconds, when it has generated sufficient power, he will switch it over to the jets. At first we shall climb slowly—comparatively slowly, I mean—but when we reach the stratosphere our speed will have risen to over ten miles per second. At this stage, as you know, we shall all suffer a temporary black-out. But it will do us no harm, and when we regain consciousness we shall have escaped from the full power of the Earth's gravity, and the rotatory jets will automatically have come into action. Do you understand?"

We said that we understood. Janet and Madge, having adjusted their safety-belts, were standing together near the radar-screens. I noticed that they were holding hands.

Bergman glanced across at me. In the artificial light a film of sweat glistened on his high forehead. "Ready, Jeremy?"

I knelt down beside the switches.

He looked at the clock. "We have," he said, "exactly ten seconds—from now. . . ."

The interior of the ship became as silent as a church. The polished central shaft gleamed brightly. Above our heads two closed doors concealed the laboratory and Madge's kitchen. Around us were the instruments, sticking out from the "walls" at awkward angles. Beneath me lay the control panel. When we took off, and the ship assumed a horizontal position, the picture would change. The doors would come naturally into place as part of the forward bulkhead. The instruments would no longer appear misplaced on the "walls" but would rest properly on the curved floor. The control panel would form the rear bulkhead, and instead of having to kneel down I could attend to it standing up, in the normal way.

Bergman was counting: "Five . . . four . . . three . . . two. . . ." Suddenly he called out: "Motor, Jeremy!"

I pressed the switch and beneath us the atomic motor burst into action, filling the compartment with a high-pitched scream. We waited. The scream rose and steadied.

"Switch to jets!" shouted Bergman.

I thrust down hard on the lever. For a moment nothing happened. Then the lights flickered and seemed to die away and a terrific roar echoed in our heads, numbing our senses. The whole ship began to tremble, as if it had lost stability. I heard Janet and Madge cry out.

"Hold on!" the professor called to us.

I clung to the protruding edge of the control panel. The "floor" shook and began to press up against the soles of my feet, as if I were being lifted by a giant's hand. Waves of sound beat round me. I felt my courage drain away.

All at once I was crushed down against the panel. I had a momentary glimpse of Janet and Madge, pale and frightened, clinging to each other. Bergman was staring in my direction, his eyes gleaming in the light.

Then all the sounds and sensations seemed to rush together in my head, as if I had been submerged in a roaring waterfall. My hand slipped from the control panel, and darkness came down in a smothering wave.

CHAPTER VI

Journey into Space

WHEN I came to myself I looked first at the clock. It was only a minute past twelve. Then I knew that our take-off had been successful, and that our journey to Hesikos had begun—three hundred thousand miles through space at an average speed of five thousand miles per hour.

The position of the ship had altered. Though the fact was not, of course, physically apparent, it was now spinning about the central shaft, giving us artificial gravitation. We had escaped from the Earth's atmosphere and were travelling so fast that the roar from the single propelling jet was being left far behind. The only sound was a continuous drone from the atomic motor, which was running at a tenth of its normal speed, driving the rotary jets and the dynamo for the lighting and instruments.

As I unbuckled my safety-belt Bergman came across and helped me to my feet. Behind him I saw Janet and Madge, patting their hair.

"Feeling better?" he asked.

"Yes. Is everything all right?"

"Of course. Quite normal."

Janet smiled at me. "Even the fact that you're last to come round, as usual!"

"Pore Jeremy," said Madge, who always seemed

able to recover quickly, " 'e needs a nice cup of tea, like we all do." She went off towards the kitchen. "I'll 'ave one ready in a jiffy."

"Thank you, dear Madge," said Bergman. He went on: "Now, Jeremy, when you feel quite fit I should like you and Janet to take over the radar and begin plotting our course. One of your tasks will be to keep careful watch for any unusual object in space. The chances against meeting any such object are about ten thousand to one—but you remember the meteors on our last journey!"

Janet shivered. "I hope that doesn't happen again!"

"I am sure it won't." The Professor looked fresh and confident enough, but somehow his quiet personality did not seem as solid and comforting as Uncle Lachlan's, gruff and irritable though that might have been. "I will divide my time between the control gauges and the navigational instruments," he continued. "As we are so short-handed I am afraid there will be very little sleep for any of us during the next sixty hours."

He turned away, walking briskly along the curved floor in the direction of the lab.

Janet and I went across to the radar. The right-hand screen, beamed on Hesikos, was blank and silent. The left-hand screen, beamed back towards the Earth, gave off a flash and a sharp pip approximately every two seconds, indicating that we were already two thousand miles from Inverard.

As we got farther away, the pips and flashes would become fainter, with more time in between. At fifty thousand miles, for example, after we had been travelling for ten hours, they would occur only once every fifty seconds. At a hundred thousand miles they would stop altogether, and the two screens would both remain blank until we got to within a hundred thousand miles of Hesikos. Then the pips and flashes would begin on the right-hand screen, at intervals of almost a hundred seconds. For about twenty hours in mid-journey we should hear and see nothing of the Earth or Hesikos, but occasionally the screens might show the Moon or one of the small asteroids as their orbits cut across our line of flight. By this means, Professor Bergman would know if we were keeping our course or not.

We sat down. I took a sheet of graph paper and a pencil and waited until Janet set the stop-watch.

At last she said: "Right, Jeremy, let's begin. First, the time—twelve-ten. That's your number *across*. Now your number *down*—two point-one-five seconds. . . . Got it?"

"Yes. Right-oh."

"I'll give you a reading every minute—to begin with at any rate. So just keep concentrating. . . ."

The hours passed. Everything went well, and our graphs developed smoothly. The drone of the atomic motor went on and on, until we scarcely noticed it. The air-pressure system was in good order and kept the compartment cool and fresh, but we got tired from want of sleep, and the tension made us all rather fed up with each other. Madge, however, gave us wonderful meals—our first lunch consisted of fried chicken and green peas—and there was plenty of tea and coffee in between. We stuck dourly to our jobs.

Then after the long blank in the middle, the right-hand screen began to show Hesikos, ninety-six thousand miles away. In less than twenty hours we should be releasing the parachute and turning to land.

I took a new sheet of graph-paper and marked down the first reading. "By now Hermanoff and Spike and Uncle Lachlan should be picking us up on their radar," I said to Janet.

"Yes—if the batteries are still working. It must be nerve-racking for them, too."

Bergman had left the controls to check the navigation in the lab., while Madge was enjoying a well-earned nap in her easy chair in the kitchen. The atmosphere in the main compartment seemed to be growing rather stuffy, and the lights shed a monotonous glare over everything. I felt sleepy, with a kind of gritty sensation behind my eyelids. The second-hand of the stop-watch was moving jerkily, coming near to the moment when we might expect another flash and pip.

Suddenly the lights flickered, and I was wide awake at once. Janet, too, looked up from the stop-watch.

The lights came on again, but above the drone of the atomic motor another sound had intruded itself —a hissing sound, faint but persistent.

"What is it?" I said, quickly.

The radar flashed again, but neither of us paid any attention. "I don't know," Janet answered. "Unless it's something to do with the air-pressure system."

"I hope it's nothing dangerous."

She listened for a moment. "I think you'd better tell Professor Bergman," she said.

When I knocked on the door of the lab. he came at once. "The pressure-system!" he exclaimed anxiously, hurrying along the curve of the hull towards the control panel. "We must look at the gauges."

I told him it had started less than a minute ago. He examined the dials. The pointer of one of them was dropping back towards zero.

"Seventeen point-four," he muttered, holding his lower lip between two stout fingers. "I was afraid of it."

Janet joined us. "Is it serious?" she asked.

"There has been a fuse, I think." Apprehension flickered in his eyes. "The oxygen is escaping faster than it is coming in. I am sorry to put it so bluntly, but unless we can repair the damage there will soon be no oxygen left in the ship."

"How soon?" I said.

"Three minutes."

Janet's face paled, and I didn't feel too good myself. But Bergman steadied us.

"Come, Jeremy—the trouble may lie in the fuse-box, behind the control panel." He bent down and opened the tool-kit. "We must unscrew the covering. You take the right-hand side. I will take the left."

I needed no second bidding. It was necessary to do something to quell the sudden fear that pounded in my heart. I thrust the screwdriver blade into the grooves of the bolts with desperate speed.

"Shall I waken Madge," whispered Janet.

Bergman shook his head. "Let her sleep. Better if she does not know what is happening."

In a few seconds the Professor and I had finished.

He levered off the metal covering and looked into the fuse-box. A row of porcelain wedges gleamed in the light, above the dark rubber of the main cable.

The air-pressure fuse was second from the right. He jerked it out, ignoring the danger of reaction if he touched an exposed element. At once I saw that the fuse wire was burnt, and rummaged in the tool-kit for a spare. Using a pair of pliers, I cut off a length of about eight inches and handed it to Bergman.

By this time he had stripped away the damaged wire. Quickly, methodically he began to fit on the spare. As he worked, however, the hissing sound above us seemed to grow louder. In a moment of panic I felt a constriction in my chest. I gasped for breath, and there was a singing in my head. Terror gripped me, but with an effort I fought against it— panting, however, in spite of myself. Then I saw that Janet and Bergman were breathing quickly, too, and that beads of perspiration stood out on their faces. I realised that we hadn't much time.

Janet jerked out: "What will happen if—if there's something else the matter besides the fuse?"

"The noise will increase," Bergman told her. "At last we shall all lose consciousness."

"But the fuse *was* damaged," I said. "That *must* have been the trouble."

Bergman had finished the re-wiring. He put his hand into the cavity, and I heard a click as he re-placed it.

"Soon now we shall know," he said. "Stay quite still, please—and listen."

The hissing became more pronounced, and we fought to find breath. The feeling of panic persisted inside me, but gradually it was dulled by a clogging lethargy. Then all at once the hissing stopped, started again, and stopped once more. In a surge of wild excitement I realised that it was easier to breathe. The pointer on the dial began to move upwards across the half-moon of figures.

"It's all right!" cried Janet, and there was a slightly hysterical edge to her voice. "The system's working again."

Bergman mopped his brow with a large white handkerchief. "Yes," he said, quietly. "It—it must have been the fuse, after all."

I didn't trust myself to speak, and it suddenly occurred to me that I had never been as scared in my life as during those last few minutes. I felt envious of Madge, who had slept through it all.

CHAPTER VII

The Green Fused Sand

THERE WAS no further trouble with the air-pressure system. Nineteen hours later my graph was almost complete, and the curved line was pointing down at a tiny circle marked "Hesikos."

We had all become very tired—and irritable, too—and I was thankful when at last Professor Bergman called us together near the control panel and announced that within the next few minutes we should be entering the atmosphere of the lost planet.

"You all know the procedure for a landing?" he said. "First I will release the parachute in the nose of the ship. Then Jeremy will shut off the rotatory jets, and as a result the ship will swing round, with its stern towards Hesikos. Finally our main jets will come into action. They will act as air-brakes, and we ought to come down lightly, cushioned by our hydraulic landing-gear."

"Shall we land anywhere near the other two ships?" asked Janet.

"About a mile away. But Dr. McKinnon and Spike and Hermanoff will already be watching us through their telescope. They will know exactly where we are going to land."

"I'm sure we'll see them just as soon as we open

the 'atch," prophesied Madge. "The pore souls—
they'll be so thankful we've come."

When the hands of the clock pointed to eleven
fifty-eight we fastened our safety-belts. At eleven
fifty-nine there was a slight tremor in the ship, as if
it had been touched by an invisible hand, and we
knew that we had come within the atmosphere of
the planet.

"Are you all ready?" inquired the Professor.

We said we were. He touched a switch and
released the parachute. The ship trembled and
began to heel over, and a pencil slid from the table
beside the radar-screens and went clattering around
the hull.

"Jeremy—rotatory jets to negative!"

I pushed over the lever, then held on grimly to one
of the instrument supports. The ship lost its spin and
began to turn at right angles. We slipped and stag-
gered as the curved hull slanted up and became the
"wall" again and the control panel sank down to
form part of a "floor" on which we could stand
upright. The door of the lab. swung open with a
crash above our heads, and instruments appeared
to protrude from the "wall" at awkward angles.
Everything was normal, I knew, but it was frighten-
ing all the same.

"Main jets, Jeremy!"

I knelt by the panel and flicked the grey switches.
The hum of the atomic motor rose to a scream, and
presently the sound of the jets came to us as we
travelled backwards into the sound. The ship
steadied, as if a careful hand had been placed beneath
us.

I watched the dial of the altimeter. Nine hundred feet . . . seven hundred . . . six hundred. . . .

Bergman was watching it, too. Suddenly he called out: "Jets off, Jeremy!"

I pressed back the switches. The thunderous screaming sounds died away, leaving behind an even more awesome silence into which there came a faint whistle of wind outside.

Three hundred feet . . . two hundred . . . one hundred. . . .

"Hold fast, everyone!"

Bergman braced himself, and we followed his example. For a moment of time which dragged on like a century the ship seemed to be suspended in a void. Madge and Janet covered their faces with their hands. Then there was a jarring thud, and an agonised hiss from the hydraulic landing-gear, and I felt a stab of pain in my legs as if I had jumped down from a great height. In a vague blur the compartment rocked and shook.

Then the ship became still. There was a complete silence, and I realised that once again we had landed safely on Hesikos

We began to unfasten our safety-belts. I had a tense feeling of excitement, and it was obvious that the others had it, too.

"Andrieff really did build a good ship!" exclaimed Janet, patting her hair and dusting the knees of her slacks.

Bergman nodded. "The important thing is that it *remains* a good ship—ready to take off again just as soon as we can re-fold the parachute." He looked round at us with a triumphant smile. He said: "Now,

Jeremy, open the main hatch, please. I will regulate the pressure system."

As I went across to the switch Madge found her voice. "Janet," she cried, her head on one side like a bird, "is my 'at on straight? I'd 'ate Dr. McKinnon to see me all mussed up."

In spite of her excitement Janet managed to smile. "It's splendid, Madge—and suits you so well, too."

The hatch rolled open with a hollow sound. We crowded to the threshold and looked out, and there below us, under a pale silvery sky, was the country-side of Hesikos just as we remembered it—a sunny, silent countryside, pale green and dotted with tufts of the little white flower which Madge had named Charity.

The horizon looked uncomfortably close to us, and I remembered that this was because Hesikos, being smaller, curved away more quickly than the Earth. The hills and the plants were oddly shaped—pointed and tall—on account of the lower gravity and more rarefied atmosphere. And the colours were clear and beautiful because the sunlight wasn't filtered as on Earth.

But none of us paid attention to these things, for almost at once we saw three figures running towards us, stumbling in their haste. I scrambled out and leaped down from the ladder. It was a jump of over twenty feet, but I landed lightly and raced to meet them. I could scarcely realise that I was seeing Uncle Lachlan and Spike and Hermanoff again.

Uncle Lachlan, who had gained a lead on his companions, was excited, too. He caught my hand and shook it hard and put his left arm about my shoulders—an unusual demonstration from a dour Scot like him.

"How are you, my boy? How are the others?"

"We're all fine." I found it difficult to speak. "Are you all right?"

"Yes. I—we thought at one time you mightn't come."

"Don't worry, Uncle Lachlan!" I camouflaged my feelings with a grin. "You and Spike and Professor Hermanoff aren't the only ones who can build space ships!"

Spike was still wearing his old windcheater and rakishly peaked cap. His mop of fair hair was as untidy as ever. "Say," he drawled, and his slow voice couldn't hide the eagerness in his eyes, "Dr. Jeremy Livingstone, I presume?"

"Hullo, Spike." I shook his hand. "Gosh, I'm glad to see you!"

"Not half as glad as I am to see you, kid! We've been following your journey on the radar and keeping our fingers crossed."

Hermanoff came panting up to join our little group. His cheeks were pale and his black pointed beard had an untended look. But there was warmth and affection in his grip on my shoulder.

"It is wonderful to see you again! To us those last few months have seemed—very long."

"I guess we all got a bit tired of one another's company," Spike confessed. "But it's okay now. I can almost smell Madge's fried steak already!"

I looked round at the green vegetation, at the trees and the quiet small rivers basking in the sun. The scent of the white flowers flowed about us, and it occurred to me that even the distant hills were offering a welcome.

"Come and meet the others," I said. "Madge will have a meal ready pretty soon—and she's baked your favourite coffee-cake, Uncle Lachlan."

"Has she now? That was kind of her." But already his thoughts were elsewhere. "Tell me, Jeremy," he went on, abruptly, "have you brought the jeep?"

"Yes, and the gelignite as you told us."

Hermanoff was smiling. "Lachlan," he butted in, "you are incorrigible! For the moment let us enjoy ourselves. Business can come later."

"Hear, hear!" approved Spike.

Uncle Lachlan rubbed his chin. "Bread before circuses?" he laughed. "Very well—so be it."

That evening, while Professor Bergman helped Madge to wash up after supper, the rest of us sat on the mossy turf at the foot of the ship's ladder and discussed our plans. The sun's disc was hanging low above the pointed hills to the south, and there was a balminess in the still air which made me feel extraordinarily happy and content.

Janet suggested that we ought to return to the Earth at once; but Uncle Lachlan shook his head.

"I thought I'd trained you better," he teased her. "What's happened to your scientific curiosity?"

"It's just that I'm scared something may happen if we stay here too long," she said. "As a matter of fact the ship's all ready to go now."

"Janet, Janet—that's no argument for a logical mind!" His lean, leathery face creased into wrinkles. "The ship will still be ready in another few weeks, and as it's now only the beginning of summer there's no danger of the ice and snow catching us this time."

"Nothing can go wrong," Spike assured her. "And I reckon when you hear of our discoveries you'll be just as keen to stay as we are."

"D'you mean about the bird?" I asked.

Uncle Lachlan nodded. "Among other things, Jeremy. . . . But first of all you should know about the bird. That was Professor Hermanoff's discovery."

"It was the first morning we opened the hatch of my ship," Hermanoff explained, spreading his hands. "The ice and snow outside were melting, and Lachlan and Spike had gone to visit the other ship, to find spare parts for the radio. While they were away I spent my time making a—what you say?— a check of the rations. After I had finished I went to the hatch to see if they were coming back, and there, perched on a rock outside, was this little bird—so tired, so weary it could not even fly when I climbed down the ladder and approached it."

"What was it like?" asked Janet.

"Like—like what you call a robin, with wings of grey and brown, and a red breast. I fed it and warmed it in my hands, and then suddenly it began to flutter its wings. I opened my hand, and very soon it flew away, back towards the south."

He pointed in the direction of the narrow hills. The lower rim of the sun seemed to be touching them now, and a flood of light, resembling a secret fire, glowed and shimmered behind them.

Uncle Lachlan spoke in a dry, scientific voice. "The inference is that it came from a warmer climate—near the equator, perhaps. Somehow it had lost its way."

"So you think there may be life, farther south?" asked Janet, quietly.

He cleared his throat. "From a study of various fossils during our first survey, Professor Bergman, Professor Hermanoff and I were convinced that once upon a time life did exist on Hesikos—abundant life. It seemed, however, that this had perished when the seasons changed and the winters became bitterly cold. But we kept in mind the possibility that nearer the equator the winters might be less severe —that life might still be going on—underground. I think that bird has proved the possibility to be a fact."

"I guess it's proof positive," Spike said.

Hermanoff agreed. "It is unlikely that there should be only one bird on Hesikos. And if there are birds, why not animals?"

"So you mean to find out at first hand, using the jeep?" said Janet.

"Yes." Uncle Lachlan was brisk and business-like again. "I had thought that Madge and Professor Bergman might stay behind in the ship, while the rest of us make a quick journey. Hesikos is quite small, and from here to the equator is only about six hundred miles. We could reach our objective in three or four days, provided there are no serious obstacles."

"Do you think—is there a chance we may find human beings?" I asked.

"If there are birds and animals at the equator, it's possible that human beings live there as well."

"Like us, you mean?"

He answered with slow deliberation. "At one time

conditions on Hesikos—climatic and otherwise—
were exactly similar to those on Earth. They would,
therefore, tend to produce living creatures like ourselves. Not only that, Jeremy. You remember the
bones we found in the cave?"

"Yes. Like a human skeleton."

"That is one significant pointer. And just the other
day, while we were waiting for you to arrive, Spike
discovered something else—something even more
extraordinary. He went by himself to climb that
ridge of hills to the south. On the other side he found
a small patch of desert, quite different from the
surrounding countryside."

"Yeah." Spike took up the story with characteristic
enthusiasm. "It was a desert that shone like glass—
that's what attracted my attention. I examined it
more closely and found it was covered with a fine
crystal sand. This sand had a greenish tinge, and
somehow it looked familiar."

His eyes were bright, and a sharp surge of excitement came to me.

"Then I remembered," he said. "I remembered
that I had seen exactly the same kind of sand in the
New Mexican desert—fused green sand caused by
the explosion of the first atomic bomb. . . ."

CHAPTER VIII

The Mark in the Cliff

I SHALL NEVER forget the thrill it gave me, that remark of Spike's about the green fused sand. I looked round at the others and thought to myself: *Is this real—or am I dreaming?* And then, as we sat there on the turf beneath the space ship, watching the sun go down behind the pointed hills of Hesikos, while Madge and Professor Bergman continued prosaically to wash dishes in the main compartment above us, Uncle Lachlan went on:

"There is only one possible conclusion to be drawn from this. As we know, Hesikos is much older than the Earth. I think that thousands of years ago, before the seasons changed, its inhabitants reached a state of civilisation similar to our own today—and finally invented the atomic bomb. Then—well, who can tell what happened afterwards? I for one should like to find out."

"Gosh, yes—so should I!" I exclaimed, involuntarily.

Uncle Lachlan smiled. "And you, Janet? Do you still think we ought to return to Earth at once?"

"No," she said, quietly. "I want to find out, too."

"All right," he said, getting up and dusting a few particles of moss from his trousers, "let's all be ready to leave first thing tomorrow morning."

Madge and Professor Bergman were naturally disappointed that they were to be left behind; but they were sensible about it, and when Spike reminded him that he would have Madge's wonderful cooking all to himself, Bergman was the first to admit that every cloud had a silver lining.

In the morning they helped us to load the jeep. To augment our tinned rations Madge put in a big parcel of cakes and sandwiches.

"And I didn't forget you, either, Professor 'Ermanoff. I found a jar which came from yore ship—caviare it is—so that's in the parcel as well, specially for you."

Besides the rations we took our sleeping-bags and a few extra clothes, along with some geological tools and sticks of gelignite. Then we climbed into the jeep—Spike at the wheel and Hermanoff beside him at the front, Janet and Uncle Lachlan and I squashed in tightly at the back.

"Take care of yourselves," Madge warned us. "And whatever you do, change your socks if you get wet. My father was a sailor, and whenever 'e went to sea my mother used to say to 'im—'Keep yore 'eart up, Albert, and always remember to change yore socks!' "

"Good advice, too!" chuckled Uncle Lachlan. "And we shan't forget. . . . You have the star-chart, Hermanoff?"

"Yes—and the sextant from my ship."

Bergman fussed around, anxiously. "Lachlan, there is just one thing. If you are in trouble please make use of your radio to get in touch with us. There might be something Madge and I could do to help."

"Very well, Lars. But I hope it won't come to that. . . . Ready, Spike?"

"Yeah, I'm ready."

"Right, start up."

The engine burst into action and we moved off across the firm turf in the direction of a dried-up river-bed. Behind us Madge and Bergman stood waving until a grove of spindly trees hid them from sight. . . .

On Hesikos daylight only lasted for nine hours, and we had to make the most of it. Spike drove fast along the river-beds and valleys, and before dark that night we had covered nearly two hundred miles. Nothing moved on the green landscape except ourselves, and the air was as fresh and warm as on an evening in June.

In places the going was rough. We hardly noticed the bumps, however, for gravity was so much less than on Earth that we seemed to float along. At first the countryside was quiet and sunny, and carpeted in green and white with patches of pink rock. But at the end of the second day, when we had done nearly four hundred miles, we saw a towering cliff in front. Next morning, after we had slept as usual in the open, an hour's drive brought us to within half a mile of it, and we stopped to discuss the situation.

"I don't like the look of it," said Spike. "There's no way up for a jeep as far as I can see."

The high wall of rock was part of the pointed ridge we had seen from the ship. It lay directly across our route to the south and seemed to stretch for miles, with no sign of a gap.

"We could leave the jeep and try to climb it," I said.

Uncle Lachlan rubbed his chin. "According to our calculations, the equator is two hundred miles farther on. It would be a pity to abandon the jeep at this stage."

Janet suggested that if we drove along at the base of the cliff we might eventually find a way across. This seemed a sensible idea, but Spike reminded us that our supply of petrol was limited and that we'd have to budget for the journey back.

"Quite so," said Uncle Lachlan. "But I think we could make a reconnaissance of about fifty miles or so and still have enough petrol left."

"Which way, though—east or west?" asked Spike.

That was the problem. The dark beetling precipice, with its serrated upper edge, looked equally impassable in both directions. Hermanoff thought we should go left, as several rock-falls were to be seen towards the east, and there was a possibility that farther on the cliff-face might have crumbled away altogether. Spike, however, disagreed with him.

"I guess it's just plain superstition," he admitted. "But if ever I come to a cross-roads my instinct always says, 'Turn right'."

"Why not toss for it?" said Janet.

But Uncle Lachlan shook his head. "If only we could get some kind of positive clue," he muttered.

It was then, as we sat there in the jeep and continued to argue, that a strange thing happened. My doubts and fears about the cliff were suddenly resolved. The others became quiet and thoughtful, too.

It seemed, however, that the definite answer to our problem had occurred only to myself. I knew what we had to do. I knew that we had to go neither to the left nor to the right but straight on towards the cliff.

"What's the matter?" Uncle Lachlan shot at me. "Suddenly thought of something?"

"Look yonder," I said. "Directly ahead of us. There's a mark in the face of the cliff, running up diagonally from the ground to the top. I didn't notice it at first, but the sun gives it a shadow now."

The others saw it at once. From this distance it looked like a grey chalk-line on a blackboard.

"But a mark in the cliff—what is the good of that?" said Hermanoff, with a frown.

"You never know," returned Spike. "If it's a ledge and happens to be wide enough, the jeep could make the gradient all right."

Uncle Lachlan nodded. "We'll go closer and have a look. Get her going, Spike."

As we approached it the sound of the jeep's engine echoed loudly against the immense cliff, which I estimated to be nearly a thousand feet high. We got out and hurried forward to examine the lower part of the "mark", and almost at once we realised that we had made a discovery of importance. It was a ledge all right, about ten feet wide. Its surface was fairly smooth, though two shallow depressions ran parallel to each other along its entire length and it was sprinkled here and there with loose stones. I couldn't help feeling that its smooth uninterrupted slope and regularity of outline were inconsistent with a natural flaw in the cliff.

Then Spike gave a startled exclamation. We looked up to where he was pointing, and there, embedded in the outer fringe of the ledge, we saw a rusty bar of metal about a foot high. We stared at it, open-mouthed and speechless, like children at a fair.

"It is incredible!" breathed Hermanoff at last. "And there are more pieces higher up—similar pieces."

"Yeah." Spike's slow drawl had deserted him. "Looks to me as if at one time there was a railing all along the outside of the ledge, right to the top."

Uncle Lachlan was nursing his chin, and I wondered if his thoughts were as filled with desperate excitement as mine. It was Janet who tried to put into words the idea that had occurred to me.

"But—but if it's metal," she said, "if it's artificial, then——"

"Then we're on the right track," put in Uncle Lachlan abruptly. "This ledge is too regular, too smooth to be natural."

"You mean——"

"I mean that once upon a time—maybe thousands of years ago—it was cut out of the cliff by the people of Hesikos and used as a road. Not a road for foot-traffic, perhaps. These two furrows could be wheel-tracks."

"But if that's true," I exclaimed, "and if there are people in Hesikos still, why don't they use it any more?"

"I don't know, Jeremy." He spoke dourly, but his eyes were gleaming. "I am hoping we may find the answer fairly soon."

Spike thought it would be possible to drive the

jeep along the ledge. "Though I wish that railing were still intact," he added. "It would be too bad if we skidded on the way!"

"I suggest we should all *walk* up to begin with," said my uncle. "If we find the road passable, then you can come back for the jeep, Spike."

"Sure.   That's the plan."

"Come then. Hermanoff and I will lead the way."

It took us only about fifteen minutes to complete the climb, and as far as one could see there was nothing to prevent the jeep from making a successful run up. On our way we kicked aside some of the larger loose stones; but as they fell out over the edge and tumbled down hundreds of feet on to the flat land below, I carefully avoided looking after them.

I haven't much of a head for heights, and by the time we reached the top I was sweating not only with exertion but also with sheer horror of the immense airy drop on our right-hand side. As we stood on the summit of the cliff, however, looking southward across another great stretch of empty country, I was determined to hide my fear and offered to help Spike in bringing up the jeep.

He looked at me narrowly. Then—"Okay," he said, briskly, "let's go. If I happen to stick anywhere you'll be useful."

Quickly we made our way down again, our steel-shod boots making an echoing din on the smooth rock. At the bottom we climbed into the jeep and Spike manoeuvred it to face the first shallow gradient of the ledge.

"You've got what it takes, Jeremy," he said, quietly. "This is going to be no cake-walk."

I looked up. Far above, like tiny puppets, Janet and Hermanoff and Uncle Lachlan were looking down at us. They were like spectators at a hill-climb—only at hill-climbs, I thought rather wistfully, dangerous parts of the track were usually protected by a stout and solid fence. . . .

Spike revved the engine. "Remember, kid, you're on the inside. If—if anything happens, bale out quick!"

"I'm not scared," I told him. "You'll do it all right."

He slammed the engine into first gear and put his foot down hard on the accelerator. The jeep lurched forward and lifted her nose to the ledge. Almost before I had time to think we were thirty or forty yards up, with the big pink rocks on the plain below beginning to look like marbles.

Spike crouched over the steering-wheel as it bucked and trembled in his hands. Small stones spurted out from beneath the tyres. Some of them struck the inner wall of the precipice and ricocheted off behind us into space. I kept looking either straight ahead or at the cliff-face whisking past eighteen inches to my left. Even when Spike remarked that we had at least two feet of clearance from the outer edge, I didn't dare glance in that direction. In my mind's eye I could see only too clearly our off-front wheel skidding away into nothingness. . . .

By Earth standards the jeep was very light, and there was plenty of wheel-spin as we climbed higher and higher. Spike and I were thrown about like cowboys at a rodeo as the tyres bumped and slithered in the ruts.

E

About half-way up we came to the worst section of the track. The surface was less smooth and the parallel furrows ran much deeper, as if they had been scoured out by water splashing from above. I held on tightly to my seat.

Then suddenly a deep hole appeared in front. I yelled a warning to Spike, but it was too late. He swerved a little, but one of the rear wheels sank into it and we stopped short, the tyre whining in a useless spin.

I offered to get out and push.

"Okay," said Spike. "But mind you don't slip and fall over the edge if the jeep starts moving."

As I slid on to the track I felt nervous and slightly sick. But I didn't give myself time to consider possibilities. I ran to the back and, taking a firm foothold, put my shoulder to the luggage grid.

"Right-oh, Spike. I'm ready."

"Okay. Take care of yourself whatever happens."

There was a drop of five hundred feet a few inches away. I was so conscious of this that it caused a kind of prickling pain, which must have been psychological rather than physical, to move along my entire right side. But the act of pushing helped to cure it.

At first it seemed that the rear wheel was stuck fast; but when Spike revved up a second time the jeep lurched out and forward. As it did so I lost my balance and fell flat on top of the hole.

That didn't worry me, however, because I remained a good distance from the edge. Besides, what I glimpsed inside the hole made me forget my fears altogether. I scrambled to my feet and raced after the jeep, which had halted some ten yards away.

As I jumped in I shouted: "There's something inside that hole!"

Spike let in the clutch. "Never mind just now. We can't stop."

"Right," I said, and my imagination was flickering like a film. "I'll tell you later."

The rest was comparatively easy; but I was thankful when we bucketed over the last few feet of the ledge and came to a stop on hard level turf at the summit. I could see that Janet, Hermanoff and Uncle Lachlan were thankful, too. In fact, Janet admitted that she had kept her eyes closed during most of our climb.

"But what caused you to stop?" asked Hermanoff. "I was afraid you might start sliding backwards."

"So was I," admitted Spike. "One wheel stuck in that hole we noticed when we climbed up first. It kept spinning and going deeper, and—well, I guess Jeremy's got something to say on that subject."

"I—we couldn't wait to make sure," I said. "But I believe that hole runs right down the middle of the road from top to bottom, though it's uncovered just at that one place. Inside there's a metal rod."

Janet stared. "A metal rod! Are you sure?"

"Yes. Rusty a bit but still strong. . . . D'you know what I think, Uncle Lachlan?"

"No."

"I think this ledge was made to take something like a tramcar. Something on rails which picked up electric power from the metal rod in the groove."

Nobody said anything else for a time. The silence of Hesikos lay around us, and from the unknown territories beyond the cliff there came the strong, unmistakable perfume of the little white flowers. Away to the right we glimpsed the silvery sparkle of a river.

It was Hermanoff who finally spoke. "If there was an atomic bomb," he said, quietly, "there would also be electricity."

Uncle Lachlan nodded. "It stands to reason. And the rails could have been embedded in those furrows we took for wheel-tracks. Being on the surface they would probably perish and disappear, but the metal rod would remain intact under the rubble."

It seemed to me the only possible explanation. I looked towards the south, half expecting to see more evidence of former life. But there was nothing. No sound or movement. Only a vast green plain bounded by another ridge of pointed hills and sprinkled with tufts of Charity, shining white beneath the rayless sun.

CHAPTER IX

Buster and Co.

THE EVIDENCE was piling up, like clues in a detective story.

There were the fossils we had collected on our first expedition—fossils which proved that millions of years ago minute sea creatures called trilobites had existed on Hesikos; and trilobites, we knew, had been the forerunners of more abundant life on Earth. Then there were the dry and brittle bones, resembling those of a skeleton, which we had discovered in the deep cave. And Professor Hermanoff's small exhausted bird. And the crystal sand. And now the iron railing and the sloping ledge.

Standing there on the top of the cliff, looking southwards, I felt suddenly that we were getting closer to the truth—closer to the mysterious power of Hesikos.

As we continued our journey in the jeep the atmosphere began to change. It grew brighter and warmer, and Spike and I took off our lumber-jackets. Beyond the next range of hills we found ourselves in a new type of country. Rocks and cliffs disappeared, and the rolling green land was irrigated by several rivers. Trees became plentiful, most of them bearing delicious fruit shaped like pears, but growing upwards like squat candlesticks.

That evening we stopped for the night beside a river. It was an odd kind of river—just a small trickle of water meandering through an expanse of white stones, with high perpendicular banks on either side.

While Janet and Spike were getting supper ready, I walked off behind a high bluff to have a dip. The water was beautifully fresh, and I splashed about enjoyably, swimming and diving for imaginary coins. When I came out and began to dress, the stones felt warm under my feet.

As I sat down to put on my shoes Uncle Lachlan appeared round the bluff and stood beside me, his hands in his pockets. He seemed quieter than usual and more relaxed.

I said something about the heat, and he reminded me that we weren't far from the equator.

"The sun got stronger all day today," he went on. "And have you noticed something else?"

"I know what you mean, Uncle Lachlan. The feeling I have is that someone is encouraging us to come on. But—we've seen nothing *alive*."

"That worries me," he admitted. "I thought that by now we should have found something—another bird perhaps, or a small animal. But they may be here. They may be watching us even now." He rubbed his chin reflectively, then continued: "You know, Jeremy, once upon a time I believed that science—Earthly science—could provide an answer to everything. Thousands of years ago Plato said that this planet exercised a peaceful influence on the world. I scoffed at the idea, believing it to be absurd. But now I'm not sure. I'm beginning to suspect that here on Hesikos there may exist a higher form of science—a science concerned with the transmission of ideas, which was old and established even before Man appeared on Earth. I used to be harsh—intolerant of ignorance. You know that, Jeremy. But I have learned a lesson. In face of the problems of Hesikos it is I who am ignorant. It is a humbling experience."

After a while I said: "Do you mean there may be people here who can read our thoughts, and send an answer to our thoughts?"

He shook his head. "I don't know, Jeremy. I just don't know. . . . But I feel we are on the verge of great discoveries—discoveries that may put our feeble human knowledge to shame."

For a time we stood by the edge of the stream, saying nothing more. The tinkle of the water was like a lullaby. We had found a mystery, but it didn't make us afraid. Rather we were looking forward to solving it, if a chance should come. There was nothing evil in Hesikos—of that we were sure—and our minds, though curious, were as peaceful as the evening air.

Quite suddenly the quietness was disturbed by Janet's voice in the distance, calling to us. "Dr. McKinnon! Jeremy! Come and see what we've found!"

She sounded both astonished and excited, and Uncle Lachlan and I raced round the bluff in her direction. We saw her kneeling down a few yards from the primus stove, with Spike and Hermanoff beside her. They all seemed to be inspecting something on the ground.

As we approached, Spike looked up and shouted: "This is it, Dr. McKinnon! Real evidence at last!"

Then I saw them—a dozen furry little animals like brown squirrels, sitting solemnly in a semi-circle. They appeared to be quite tame, too; and one, with a bushy white tail arched above his head, was hopping across the mossy turf towards Janet.

As we joined the others Uncle Lachlan said quietly: "Yes—living and warm-blooded. . . . I have been waiting for this."

I stared at the small animals with my mouth open. They looked lively and well fed, and as they sat there on their haunches, forepaws held together beneath their chins, they kept up a slow chirruping.

"It is amazing," said Hermanoff. "They were drinking at the river and did not seem to notice us at first. But when Janet called they came immediately to make friends."

Spike picked up the one with the bushy tail. "Say, he's real cute. . . . That's right, sit up on my arm, Buster. How's tricks?"

Buster chirruped loudly and clapped his forepaws together.

"I guess he understands," grinned Spike.

"I'm sure he knows that at any rate we're friends," said Janet. "Let's try him with some sugar."

She took a lump from the pocket of her slacks and held it out to him, but oddly enough he seemed not to notice it at first. When she put it into his paw, however, he caught it tightly, though clearly still at a loss to understand its purpose.

"Go on," said Spike, tickling the small alert ears. "It's good to eat."

Buster glanced in his direction, then with sudden energy began to crunch the sugar in his sharp white teeth. I couldn't help laughing at how he smacked his lips after each bite. It was obvious that he was enjoying himself.

Uncle Lachlan had been studying him intently. All at once he said: "Let me have him for a moment."

Spike was surprised by my uncle's serious tone. But he spoke gently to Buster: "Come on—move over, chum. Dr. McKinnon wants you."

Taking him on his hand, Uncle Lachlan looked closely into the little creature's face. Finally he said: "I have been noticing his eyes. The others are the same, too."

Hermanoff nodded. "I know what you mean, Lachlan. I observed it from the beginning."

"What about his eyes?" I said.

Uncle Lachlan waved his finger less than an inch from Buster's nose. "You see—he pays no attention. He didn't know about the sugar, either, until Janet put it in his paw."

A small still air of tragedy seemed to float around us. Spike said: "What are you getting at, Dr. McKinnon?"

Gently my uncle stroked Buster's fur. "If I'm not mistaken these little animals are all quite blind."

Janet gave an exclamation. "But—but why should they be blind?" she cried. "Is there any reason?"

"They may live underground—except at certain seasons, when they come out to drink. What's your opinion, Hermanoff?"

"The same as yours. The eyes are there, open and apparently healthy. But if these animals lived in the

dark for many generations, they would lose the power
of sight."

"Poor little things!" said Janet. "Yet they seem
to be quite happy."

"If they have never known what it is to see,"
returned Uncle Lachlan, "then blindness to them is
natural."

There was such pity in my heart for Buster and his
friends that I felt like crying. They were so innocent
and friendly that their blindness seemed cruelly
unjust. But we had to accept the fact, and soon—in a
kind of emotional reaction—we started to feed them
all on lumps of sugar.

They sat round us, happy and excited, nibbling for
dear life. Janet called them "brownies", after the
colour of their coats; but I thought the name appro-
priate in another way, too. The small, ghostly
brownies which are supposed to haunt the ancient
castles of Scotland have the reputation of being
sharp and clever. The brownies of Hesikos were
just the same; and sometimes it seemed to me that
they could actually read our thoughts and offer
comments in their own language of chirrups and
squeaks.

When the sun touched the horizon, however, they
seemed suddenly to lose confidence, and as dusk
spread over the countryside they scampered off towards a pointed hill, some miles away to our left. It
got dark quickly, and we couldn't see exactly where
they went; but that night, lying in my sleeping-bag
under the steady light of the stars, I kept wondering
about the pointed hill. Something about it had
struck me as peculiar. I couldn't think what.

In the morning, as we ate our porridge and tinned milk, we were surprised and thrilled to witness more evidence of life. It came to us first as an unusual sound—unusual, that is, on Hesikos, where everything was as silent as a church; the sound of birds calling, high above our heads.

We looked up and saw them, their white wings flashing in the sun. I counted about a score, all flying towards the south.

Spike said quickly: "I guess they're a lot bigger than the one you saw, Professor Hermanoff?"

"Much bigger—yes. My little bird was like a robin. Those are the size of seagulls."

They passed over into the eye of the sun, their cries receding to a plaintive whisper. I wondered why they appeared to be so excited, why they were flying so fast. It was as if something had frightened them, farther north.

"They're landing on the hill," said Janet, shading her eyes. "Where the brownies went last night."

"I think we should investigate that hill," replied Uncle Lachlan, slowly. "The jeep will take us there in a few minutes. There's something odd about it. Half-way up there's a kind of terrace, and what looks like an archway in the rock."

We all had a look at the place through the binoculars, but the sun was shining into our eyes, and it was impossible to make out details. Were the terrace and the archway artificial, I wondered—or had they been formed by a natural process of erosion?

We finished our breakfast and began to pack up. We had slept in a sheltered nook below the bank of the stream, and our route to the hill lay first along the stone-strewn river-bed and then up a kind of corrie about half a mile farther on.

Hermanoff paused in the act of rolling up his sleeping-bag. "There is something else that has been exercising my mind," he said, abruptly. "These valleys, with the high banks on either side—like the one we are in now—no vegetation grows in them. They are rocky and bare, as if great rivers have been running through them. And yet we find only a little stream, like this one."

"Yes," said Uncle Lachlan. "And stranger still, there's no river-weed, and no fish."

Janet suggested that they might have been scoured out by glaciers, millions of years ago.

But Hermanoff was dubious. "The stones are too fresh—too clean and bare," he said.

It was then, as we paused in our work to ponder this new problem, that Spike turned suddenly and looked towards the north, far up the valley.

"D'you hear anything?" he asked.

For a moment we stood motionless, listening. Then I did hear it, and so did the others. An ominous roar, gradually becoming louder.

To our dismay, the ground began to tremble beneath our feet.

CHAPTER X

The Tunnel

"JEREMY—THE binoculars!"

Uncle Lachlan snatched them from me and looked in the direction of the sound. Far up the valley —and hemmed in by its precipitous sides—I saw a heaving brown mass moving quickly towards us. It was flecked with white.

"I should have known!" he exclaimed. "Quick— into the jeep everyone! Start up, Spike!"

"But the sleeping-bags!" cried Janet. "The tins of food——"

"Leave them behind. We haven't a moment to lose."

The sound was coming nearer; but I don't think any of us, except Uncle Lachlan, fully understood its cause. We obeyed his order, however, and scrambled into the jeep, bumping against one another in our haste.

"Which way?" said Spike, pressing the starter.

"Straight down the river-bed. Then sharp left up the corrie—and along to the hill where the brownies went."

The jeep lurched off through the gears, its tyres pounding on the smooth white stones. I remember that my back was wedged hard against the corner of a water-can. Because of this, and by reason of the excitement and hurry, I found it difficult to breathe.

Janet was beside me, trying to look back over her shoulder. "But, Dr. McKinnon," she gasped out, "what is it?"

He didn't answer. Then I felt her stiffen and grow rigid, and at the same moment I also understood the danger that had come to us.

A mile away, and quickly approaching the place where we had spent the night, a great volume of water was pouring after us, filling the valley to a depth of almost a hundred feet. Its yeasty brown crest leaped along the banks, at times rearing up and spilling over them. At the speed it was travelling it would catch us up in a matter of seconds; and if by then we hadn't got out of the valley we should be overwhelmed and drowned. Somewhere at the back of my mind was a picture—a Biblical painting of the Israelites crossing the Red Sea on dry land and the pursuing Egyptian chariots being engulfed by a great wall of falling water.

I jerked out: "Can we get clear in time?"

The lines on Uncle Lachlan's face, touched by the bright morning sun, seemed to be far more deeply etched than usual. But he sounded matter-of-fact and steady. "I think so, Jeremy—if the jeep keeps moving. We'll be safe on the high terrace."

Hermanoff, too, had been looking back. As if from a distance I heard his voice: "I understand it now. Every few months it happens, after the melting of the snow and ice. Somewhere in the north the water piles up, dammed by broken ice and debris. Then suddenly it bursts out and comes sweeping down the river-beds. No wonder nothing grows in the valleys—and fish could never live in these conditions."

Spike said something about the birds. His idea was that they had become aware of the approaching flood and that when we saw them they had been flying back to the safety of their home-ground. But just then cool scientific explanations seemed unimportant. The main impression in our minds was that though the jeep was hurtling along at fifty miles an hour the flood was rapidly gaining on us.

Uncle Lachlan, however, did not seem to be unduly worried. "We're all right," he said. "We're well ahead. . . ."

Then a shallow corrie opened out to our left— the corrie which would lead us to safety on the high terrace above the valley. It looked steep, and its earthy slope was sprinkled with loose stones, but I had confidence in Spike and in the jeep's engine. A sense of relief came over me, and I felt that Janet, too, was beginning to relax.

Spike changed down like a racing-driver, swerved to the left and set the jeep's nose at the gradient. Half a mile behind us the flood was roaring along the valley, obliterating the white stones and the glinting surface of the little stream. But we were escaping—we should soon be clear of its menacing power. I yelled encouragement to Spike and grinned at Uncle Lachlan.

There was a sudden crack of breaking metal. With a sickening skid the jeep came to a stop, spread-eagled against the surface of the corrie. The engine roared. Next moment it stalled and was silent, and the thunder of the flood filled our ears.

"Spike—what's happened?" shouted Uncle Lachlan.

"Back axle's gone. That hidden rock. . . . We're finished!"

There was hopeless desperation in Spike's answer, but Uncle Lachlan ignored it. "Get out—all of you!" he commanded. "Run for your lives—up this bank and on to the terrace!"

We tumbled out.

"The stores!" cried Hermanoff.

"Grab anything you can!" Uncle Lachlan himself reached for the sextant. "Quick—the flood will be on us in half a minute now!"

I snatched up a tin box lying on the back seat. At the time I hadn't the slightest idea what it was. As I turned to follow the others my jersey caught in the handle of one of the doors. I wrenched it free, leaving strands of wool hanging from a jagged tear.

I caught up with Spike, who was gripping Janet's hand and helping her on. In front of them Uncle Lachlan and Hermanoff were panting up the slope. At each step forward we slipped back about a foot. Small stones rolled and slithered beneath us. To me it was like a nightmare, and a swelling lump of terror clogged my throat.

The flood was now only four hundred yards away, wallowing and crashing round a bend in the valley. The ground was shaking, and if we wanted to speak we had to scream above the noise. As I glanced back I realised that we were still thirty feet below the level of its crest. Could we reach the terrace in time?

Janet was sobbing with exertion and fear. But

Spike, as strong as a pony, kept pulling her after him. I plugged on immediately behind, with the sweat running down into my eyes. The sliding stones of the corrie turned into a pale blur.

Then, just in front, I saw Hermanoff sink to his knees. I heard him say: "Leave me, Lachlan! I cannot go on!"

But my uncle jerked him to his feet. "You can, Hermanoff! You can! Don't give up!" He looked across at me and shouted: "Take his other arm, Jeremy! Quickly!"

The flood was almost on us. I took Hermanoff's right arm and glanced up and found that the terrace was now only ten feet above. With a final burst of energy I dragged him behind me, and as the first splash struck my burning face we heaved ourselves over the summit and lay panting on the dry mossy ground above the corrie. I felt water pouring across my feet; but as I regained my breath and looked round, it came to me that the flood had passed us by and we were safe.

I noticed that Janet was clinging to Spike, her face hidden against his shoulder. Hermanoff was muttering: "You saved my life, Lachlan—you and Jeremy. . . ."

My uncle sat up and tried to sound light-hearted. "Nonsense, Hermanoff! You came up that bank like a steeplechaser. I hope I'll be as spry as you are when I'm fifty!"

Presently, with the brown water surging past only a few inches below us, we began to feel better. Janet moved apart from Spike and began to tidy her hair.

F

"What's worrying me is the jeep," I said, "miles below all that water."

Grimly Spike nodded. "If ever we find it again there won't be much of it left, I reckon."

Uncle Lachlan, however, was more optimistic. "I don't think this flood will last for more than a few hours. We may be able to salvage it. . . . By the way," he added, "what *did* we manage to save? Everybody grabbed something, didn't they?"

We spread our treasures on the turf. It proved to be a strange collection, and we couldn't help laughing at some of the items. Janet, for instance, put down a box of dates, while Hermanoff, with a rueful smile, displayed a packet of his own cheroots.

Spike grinned. "You weren't as darned silly as I was, Professor. I picked up a bag, thinking it was food. Now it turns out to be gelignite!"

"I took the sextant and the star-chart," said Uncle Lachlan. "A kind of scientific instinct, I suppose. What about you, Jeremy?"

"I took the tin with the green label. It happens to contain the concentrated food tablets, but at the time I didn't really know what it was."

He patted my shoulder. "That's not so bad. These tablets will keep us all alive for a fortnight at least. And we shan't go thirsty. There's plenty of water, in all conscience!"

We packed the stuff into a bag, which Spike said he would look after, and for a time we discussed our next move. This was obviously to get back to the ship as quickly as we could; but there was one grave problem. Would our food tablets—and one box of dates—be enough to sustain us during a walk of six hundred miles?

As we recovered from the horror of our experience we got up and looked about. Behind us was the pointed hill, and below its peak—just above the terrace on which we stood—was a dark opening. I knew at once it was the "archway" that Uncle Lachlan had seen through the binoculars.

And then, for the time being at any rate, we forgot to be uneasy and afraid. As we went towards the opening and stopped outside, we realised that it actually was artificial and formed the entrance to a tunnel cut out of the solid rock. Again I felt a thrill of anticipation creeping along my spine.

Spike peered in. "Not much doubt about it," he said. "This place has been made with tools—or explosives."

"I agree." Uncle Lachlan's eyes were alert. "Though the walls at the entrance here are so weathered and smooth that thousands of years have probably passed since it was done."

The floor sloped down quite steeply, I saw, at an angle of nearly forty-five degrees. It seemed to go in for a long way, too.

"There is one thing significant," said Hermanoff. "The mouth is well above the level of the floods."

High in the face of the mountain above our heads were a dozen smaller holes, each about a foot in diameter. It occurred to me that they might be used by the brownies on the approach of winter, or when a flood was coming. Uncle Lachlan was of the same opinion, and he thought that the birds might probably take refuge in them as well.

But the big tunnel was what interested us most. I suggested that we should go inside and explore it.

"Yes. But I don't think we should *all* go in—to begin with at any rate," said Uncle Lachlan.

Janet asked why.

"Well"—he sounded slightly hesitant—"it's a matter of common sense. Two's enough for a reconnaissance."

"You believe there may be danger?" said Hermanoff.

"No—not necessarily. But there's a military adage that one should never risk one's whole force on a doubtful mission. Jeremy and I will go. If we don't come back within, say, half an hour, you may come and look for us."

Spike was inclined to argue, but Uncle Lachlan put a hand on his arm and said quietly: "I should like you to stay with Janet and Hermanoff. You are our engineer. If—if anything should happen, you will be more valuable to the party than either Jeremy or myself."

"Aw, heck—that's a darned cold-blooded way of looking at it!"

"It's common sense, Spike, as I said."

He tucked his arm in mine, and we went into the cavern. Janet called after us: "Don't do anything rash—please!"

I had a torch in my pocket, which was lucky, and as we went farther in it proved extremely useful. The circle of light which marked the mouth of the tunnel became smaller and smaller behind us, and finally, when we had gone about four hundred yards, it disappeared altogether.

Strangely enough, the air remained fresh, and after a time we found that the floor no longer sloped downwards but was almost level.

At last I said: "You know, Uncle Lachlan, this tunnel gives me a queer feeling."

"What kind of feeling?"

"As if it were being *used*—used and looked after. It's so clean and fresh somehow."

"You're quite right," he answered. "Ordinarily at this depth the walls would be slimy and damp."

I was throwing the beam of the torch in front, and suddenly it picked out a hole in the wall. It was about two feet wide, situated a yard above the floor. We went forward to examine it and found that it curved straight down.

Uncle Lachlan rubbed his chin. "Like a ventilator shaft," he said. "This may account for the fresh air and dry walls."

Then we heard it, coming up the shaft—a throbbing, humming noise which, even as we listened, rose and fell and died away again.

The hair prickled on the back of my neck. I said to Uncle Lachlan: "What d'you think it is?"

For a moment he didn't reply. Then he put his hand on my shoulder. "I'm not sure," he answered, quietly. "But if I heard it anywhere else I'd say it was the sound of a huge dynamo. . . ."

CHAPTER XI

The Opening Door

IN THE long dark tunnel Uncle Lachlan's voice echoed away in a whisper: "If I heard it anywhere else I'd say it was the sound of a huge dynamo."

I felt cold, as one often does in moments of intense excitement. "But—but there can't be a dynamo down there!" I said.

"There's power, Jeremy—power of some kind." As he spoke the humming noise reached us again, throbbing in our ears and then once more sinking into silence. "Notice how it's coming up the shaft in irregular waves. You can feel a current of air, too."

"It's as if there was something *living*—hundreds of feet below us here."

"I think there *is* life. But what kind of life we cannot tell—as yet."

We went on again. I was afraid to go on, but at the same time no one could have persuaded me to go back. There was a mystery here—a mystery which just had to be solved. It made me afraid, but it fascinated me, too, like the hooded eyes of a snake.

We had told the others that if we didn't return to the mouth of the tunnel in half an hour they were to come after us; and as we continued our journey, down and down into the dark, we soon realised that we couldn't possibly be back in time. About half an hour had gone by when my torch flashed against what seemed to be the end of the tunnel—a flat dusty surface like the bottom of a tumbler.

It was very quiet now. The sound we had heard had completely disappeared, and as we stared at the solid barrier confronting us, I had a feeling of sharp disappointment.

But Uncle Lachlan didn't appear to be disappointed. "That's odd," he said, his words fluttering in the high roof like birds. "If this tunnel has been cut out artificially why should it come to a dead stop here?"

He took the torch from me and went closer to the barrier. "M'm—odder still" he remarked. "The flat surface doesn't seem to fit properly. There's a kind of narrow chink all round, between it and the walls."

Finally he struck it with the butt of the torch, and once again excitement tingled through every vein in my body, for the dusty surface gave out a metallic clang.

"Gosh," I exclaimed, "it's hollow!"

He was excited, too. I could sense it, though when he spoke his voice remained dry and precise. "This," he said, "becomes more and more interesting!" Then he added: "I'm almost sure of it, Jeremy. It's a great iron door, sealing off what's behind it from the outer part of the tunnel."

"But why?" I blurted out. "What does it mean?"

He pointed to the floor, and I saw that the barrier rested in a slot in the stone. "If I'm not mistaken," he said, "it's actually a flat piece of iron shaped like a wheel. It may open by rolling sideways along that groove."

"There's no way of opening it," I answered. "From this side at any rate."

He nodded, flicking the torch. "Quite so. But remember that Spike has a few sticks of gelignite."

"So he has. I forgot."

He tapped the iron barrier again, and I heard him muttering to himself. "What is its purpose, I wonder? It's like the Sphinx—blank and inscrutable. . . ."

And then I almost jumped out of my skin, for suddenly behind the iron door, I heard a sharp click and the low hum of a motor. Uncle Lachlan stepped back and put his arm around my shoulders. I could feel him trembling a little. The humming noise rose to a high pitch. The door moved. Crunching and rumbling, it began slowly to roll sideways, and the reverberations echoed in my head like thunder.

Uncle Lachlan's fingers bit into my right arm. It was obvious that the movement of the door was controlled by the unseen motor, which I was sure must be electric; but at the time the mechanics of the thing seemed of minor importance. It was what we saw behind the door that riveted our attention.

At first it was a light—a beautiful silvery light. Then it was something else—something which lay like a dream beyond the end of the tunnel.

"Uncle Lachlan," I said. "What have we found?"

His fingers tightened. "The secret of Hesikos, I think."

The door was fully open now. There was another click and the whine of the motor died away. But we remained motionless, scarcely daring to breathe.

Uncle Lachlan whispered: "At last, Jeremy—at last! But I never imagined anything like this!"

We stood there in a maze, looking down through the tunnel towards a city—a small city of quiet streets and white houses, built far under the surface of the planet. High above it was a great curved dome of solid white rock. A soft silvery light made the whole picture seem like one out of fairyland. As we watched we saw movement in some of the narrower streets to the left, as if people were walking there.

I can't describe my feelings. I was excited and afraid and triumphant all at the one time, and in spite of his sober self-discipline I knew that my uncle was the same.

"If we go in there," I said, at last, "the door may shut behind us."

"I'd thought of that," he answered. "Perhaps we should wait for the others."

But as he spoke the same thought occurred to both of us—a thought of startling clearness.

The thought was like a voice: "Do not be afraid," it seemed to say. "The door has opened in welcome. It will remain open for your friends. Come at once —and do not be afraid."

"It's strange," I said. "When this kind of thing happens I always feel better, and not scared any more."

He nodded and smiled. "That really was a welcome. I think we should accept it."

The white buildings, delicately pillared like old Greek temples, looked almost too beautiful to be true. As we walked down towards them along the tunnel, we saw that they were surrounded by a white wall. In this wall, leading through into the widest of the streets, was a gate made of shining metal.

When we descended to the level of the city the wall concealed the buildings from us. Of one thing, however, we were certain. There was nothing evil behind the wall. We could both feel it. I remembered the first time we had landed on Hesikos and the feeling that had come to us of peace and quiet and friendliness. This was the same. It was as if someone were *telling* us that we had nothing to fear.

Abruptly my uncle said: "You know, Jeremy, I believe we are on the verge of astonishing things—discoveries only imagined by our Earthly science."

"You mean this underground city and the silvery light?"

"No. There are underground cities on earth—cities of refuge from enemy bombs. And concealed lighting is commonplace, too. During the War we directed hidden searchlights on to the clouds and created artificial moonlight for our troops. Something like that is happening here—lights reflected from the great white dome, high up there above the city. . . . No, I don't mean physical things, Jeremy. I mean the power of communication between one mind and another. . . ."

I was about to ask another question when I noticed that the shining gate, now only fifty yards away, had opened. Then we halted in amazement, for in the gateway there appeared a crowd of people —a crowd of nearly fifty, perhaps—all dressed in tunics and knee-length garments not unlike my shorts, with sandals on their bare legs. We heard the murmur of their talk, and I remarked how tall they were.

"Tall—yes. Like the trees and the narrow hills." Uncle Lachlan sounded thoughtful as we moved forward again. "Two of them are coming to meet us," he went on. "A man and a girl."

The man was middle-aged, with a blond beard and a mass of fair hair swept back from his forehead. The girl was slight and slender—though nearly as tall as the man—and her golden hair hung to her shoulders, in vivid contrast with the snowy whiteness of her tunic.

I heard my uncle murmuring to himself. "So fair, divinely fair. . . ." Then he straightened his shoulders and smiled, as if suddenly remembering that he was by profession a scientist and by upbringing a canny Scot. "We must seem odd-looking creatures to them!" he remarked. "But keep your courage, Jeremy. Remember that you and I are personalities, too—divinely made, with thoughts and opinions of our own."

As we approached, we saw that the man and the girl were smiling. They were both pale, and the skin on their high cheekbones seemed almost transparent. It wasn't the transparency of illness, however, but of superb mental and physical health. I began to be conscious of my own rough red hair and ugly freckles.

At a few yards' distance we stopped and faced one another.

The man bowed slightly. "Welcome, my friends— welcome to Hesikos. We have waited long for this moment."

"Sir," said Uncle Lachlan, "you are very kind."

"My name is Solveg, Dr. McKinnon." His voice was deeply resonant and filled with authority, yet it also had a quality of kindness which touched my heart. "I am the head of my people," he went on, "and this girl is my daughter, Asa."

Asa was looking at me with clear blue eyes—the bluest I have ever seen. "I am glad you have come," she said, warmly. "It is interesting to *see* you, Jeremy."

I goggled at her, in the rudest possible way; and instead of saying something complimentary in return all I could blurt out was: "But—but how do you know our names? How can you speak English?"

"My father will tell you later," she smiled. "Meanwhile you must both come to our house. You have been in danger from the flood, and are tired. When you have bathed and eaten you will learn all there is to know."

"Yes. Come, Dr. McKinnon." Solveg gestured towards the gate and the interested crowd. "You and I shall lead the way. Asa will bring your nephew."

For a moment Uncle Lachlan looked worried. "Thank you," he returned, with a dignity which I admired. "But we have friends coming behind us. Shouldn't we first go back and fetch them?"

Solveg shook his head. "It is unnecessary. Janet and Spike and Professor Hermanoff have already been—informed. Petra, my chief lieutenant, will greet them when they come and bring them to *his* house."

"Very well. Let us go." My uncle fell into step. "There are a thousand questions I want to ask."

"I can sense them," smiled Solveg. "It is a pleasure to make contact with a lively mind like yours."

Asa and I followed them, about ten paces behind.

"And I want to ask *you* a thousand questions, Jeremy!" She was looking up at my face in a way which ought to have been embarrassing, but somehow wasn't. "For instance, you see that my hair is smooth and fair, like all the people of Hesikos. But yours is thick and red. Have boys on Earth all got red hair?"

"Oh, no," I answered, doing my best to sound light-hearted and at ease. "Only the unfortunate ones like me! It never lies down unless I put oil on it."

"Unfortunate?" she said, as if puzzled. "I do not think you are unfortunate to have red hair. I like it very much. . . . And the little brown marks on your face—what are they?"

"If they're not just spots of dirt I expect they're freckles."

"What are freckles?"

When you think of it, that was rather a poser. "I—I don't exactly know," I confessed. "But they're caused by the sun."

"I see." She seemed to grow thoughtful. "I wish I had freckles, too. We are all pale in Hesikos, as you may have noticed, because we scarcely ever see the sun." Then she laughed and squeezed my arm. "Oh, but I am sorry, Jeremy. I shouldn't be asking questions. Not now at any rate. After our meal, perhaps. I'm so excited *seeing* you—that's the trouble. . . ."

CHAPTER XII

Secrets of Ancient Time

WE PASSED in by the gateway, where the people of the city stood smiling and waving. Solveg and Asa wore white, which was perhaps a sign of rank, but the others had tunics of red and green and purple.

I tried to appear polite and friendly, especially to the thin and rather delicate looking children who kept staring at my disreputable jersey and shorts. I could feel they were surprised at how broad I was compared with themselves. Asa seemed far stronger and sturdier than most.

Inside the gate we found ourselves in a wide street paved with warm pink stone. What struck me at once was the cleanness and freshness of the place. There was no dirt or dust, no smell of smoke or petrol, and though we were several thousand feet underground I could detect no trace of stuffiness. The houses on either side were small but bright and airy, and, as one might have expected in an underground city where the humidity and temperature of the atmosphere was mechanically regulated, there was no glass in the windows. Outside many of the front doors were little gardens containing flowers and fruit trees, and in almost every case there was at least one plant of Charity.

Uncle Lachlan and I were taken to an unusually large house, built of pink and white stone, and there we had a wonderful warm plunge. The bath was simply a depression in the stone floor—rather like the kind you see in pictures of ancient Rome— with a shining lever at one end to regulate the temperature. There was something in the water, I'm sure, for when I came out I felt greatly refreshed and as fit as a fiddle.

Afterwards, sitting on couches made of plaited fibre, we had a meal with Solveg and Asa. This consisted of delicious cakes, with a soft coating like honey, and a drink which tasted like the pear-shaped fruit we had found on our first visit to Hesikos.

When we had finished Asa and I sat listening to her father and Uncle Lachlan as they talked. By now, what with the bath and the delightful food, I had lost my sense of uneasiness. Curiosity was the feeling uppermost in my mind. What was the story behind this secret city?

Uncle Lachlan put the question.

"As you have guessed," Solveg replied, "the history of our planet extends back for millions of years. We were a civilised race long before the creation of Man. But even then we knew that one day creatures like ourselves would appear on Earth. Your atmosphere was the same as ours—with oxygen, nitrogen and carbon monoxide—and every condition favoured human life. Throughout the centuries our many scientific inventions have enabled us to keep Earth and its development under close observation."

"You had the atomic bomb, I think? We found a

patch of green crystal sand in your northern hemisphere."

Solveg inclined his head. "Our first atomic bomb was made a hundred thousand years ago—in what we now call 'The Dark Age of Hesikos.' Our civilisation at that time was exactly similar to yours on Earth today."

"A dark age, you said?"

"Yes, Dr. McKinnon. And in the end our atomic weapons destroyed the face of Hesikos and disturbed its motion round the sun. The bitter winters came, and only a few were able to survive by constructing this city in the rock. It was the same with the birds and animals."

"I see." Uncle Lachlan's attitude was one of well-mannered interest, but his bony fingers, I saw, were clasped tensely together about one knee. "Then your people didn't actually *lose* their knowledge of science?"

"No. But in due course great prophets were born—prophets who showed how it could be harnessed in the cause of good. All weapons and explosives were forbidden, and the formulae for their manufacture destroyed. Only the ancient knowledge of electricity was retained, and this merely because it provides the light and heat which makes life here possible. Our ancestors developed a new branch of science—the science of the mind. They learned how to transmit thoughts and ideas to one another, without speech, until at last, under certain conditions, they could communicate with other minds outside Hesikos."

"Then Plato was right!" said my uncle. "When Hesikos circled near the earth, thousands of years ago, your ancestors were above to exercise a power for peace?"

"That is true, though unfortunately the influence could be transmitted only for a short period, while the planets were close to each other." Solveg paused to drain his cup, then continued: "In those days our scientists invented an instrument that we still use—you will see it at another time, Dr. McKinnon. We call it the Electronome, and it is built on the principle of your radar, though I am afraid that, as yet, you have insufficient knowledge to understand in detail how it works. But in simple terms its function is to magnify the power of our thoughts, so that they may travel for long distances through space. It also receives messages in return."

At this point, quite involuntarily, I butted in. "Does this—does the Electronome account for the strange thoughts and ideas that sometimes come to us —like a voice inside our heads?"

Solveg bowed. "Yes, Jeremy. When you and your friends arrived here first we discovered by experiment the wavelength of your thoughts, and ever since we have been able to follow them—and to offer help if you were in danger or doubt."

"That is also why we know your names—and what has been happning to you," said Asa.

"I can follow that," I replied. "But I still don't understand how you speak English!"

Solveg was clearly amused by my rather blunt comments. "You have a mind like your uncle," he remarked. "A persistent mind. I think one day you will be a great scientist, by Earthly standards. And who knows—you may even be the first to convey to

G

Man's limited intelligence the rudiments of our science here. But I wonder if at the age of seventeen you will be able to understand my answer to your question?"

"At seventeen," I said, "we understand a lot more than people give us credit for."

"That, I think, is true." He regarded me closely, his thin, clever face looking sombre and solemn. Then he went on: "At any rate I will try to explain. The fact is, I am not speaking at all. I am transferring my thoughts to your mind. Thoughts have no specific language. They are universal. But as you receive them from me, you unconsciously translate them into English, which is your native tongue. Professor Hermanoff would imagine I was speaking to him in a European language."

"But, sir—I can *hear* what you say."

"It is a mental illusion. With Asa and myself it works in reverse. We know you are making sounds with your mouth, but we disregard them. We concentrate on receiving the ideas behind your words."

I was trying hard to work it out. The struggle must have shown on my face, for all of a sudden Asa burst out laughing.

"Don't look so puzzled!" she said. "It's just something that happens. You don't need to worry about the whys and wherefores."

I ran my fingers through my hair. "I thought radar was pretty complicated, but this beats it hollow!"

Solveg patted my shoulder. "Indeed it does, Jeremy. But"—he chuckled—"please don't regard

Asa and myself as complicated radar sets! In spite
of our knowledge we are still human beings, with
the same essential emotions as you and your Uncle
Lachlan. We even pride ourselves on having a sense
of humour."

My uncle clasped his fingers still tighter about
his knee. "I am glad of that, Solveg. We could feel
that you were kind and good, but a sense of humour is
the one thing we didn't expect in people of another
world. . . . Now," he added, "what of your mode of
life—your philosophy?"

"We are, of course, vegetarians," replied Solveg.
"We live on food manufactured from the fruits and
vegetables gathered above ground every three
months. In regard to education, we have a school
and a college, and every child has to be proficient in
three subjects—electrical engineering, mental
science and the ancient history of Hesikos. Afterwards, according to merit, each individual is
appointed to a special occupation—as an electrician,
for instance, or a food producer, as a miner or a
street-cleaner. Perhaps he becomes a teacher or a
physician. And because the number of our popu-
lation is carefully controlled, no one has either
too much or too little to do."

Solveg paused. Outside the house it was very
quiet, but in the distance I thought I heard Spike's
voice. After a moment our host continued: "As to
our philosophy, Dr. McKinnon, we are resigned to
the eventual decay of our planet. There is no con-
flict in our small world here. We have banished
evil, and our creed is one of constant charity and
good will."

This was getting a bit beyond me, but I noticed that Uncle Lachlan's expression had changed. To my surprise, lines of annoyance gathered on his forehead.

Abruptly he said: "I admire your creed, Solveg. But if you don't mind me saying so, your philosophy irritates me intensely. It contains a flaw."

"A flaw?" Solveg didn't sound at all resentful, but rather amused. "You, with your limited intelligence, you dare to criticise our philosophy?"

"I do," replied Uncle Lachlan, in the dour voice I knew so well. "Your ancestors faced evil things and changed them into good. But now—in this secret city—you are hiding from evil, like ostriches with their heads in the sand. You are afraid to emerge and create a new world. You are afraid to use explosives and atomic power—not for evil but for good. You are resigned to death and decay for Hesikos, but with your power and knowledge you could people the whole planet with a sturdy new race—men of good will who could reach out and help other worlds, not only spiritually but also in more practical ways. . . . No, Solveg," he said, with grim vehemence, "in my humble opinion any philosophy which refuses to acknowledge evil—and to face up to it—is a barren philosophy. How can you know what is good when you are ignorant of what is bad?"

I was worried in case Solveg might be angered by this outburst. But I soon saw that he was giving the argument deep consideration. After a time he looked up.

"Dr. McKinnon," he said, "I have always believed that my people were infinitely wiser, infinitely

superior to the people of the Earth. I still think that
we can teach you many things; but now my mind is
troubled. It may be that *you* have something to
teach *us*."

"I hope so," retorted my uncle. "For the sake of
Hesikos and the whole universe."

Solveg was about to speak again, when Asa,
jumping up from her couch, lightly interrupted him.
"Oh, Father, aren't we becoming too serious?
Jeremy's brain will boil over if he tries to understand
any more!"

I grinned, relieved that the tension should be
broken. "It's just about blown the lid off already!"
I said.

"Poor Jeremy!" Solveg was warm and kind again.
"But Dr. McKinnon and I have really only begun
our discussion. . . . Asa," he went on, "perhaps you
would take Jeremy and show him the main dynamo
and the Electronome?"

She clapped her hands. "That's a good idea.
We'll call for Janet and Spike, too—at Petra's
house."

"And ask Professor Hermanoff to join us here."

"Very well, Father."

"I have a feeling that Dr. McKinnon and I are
going to have a long argument, and he may be able
to hold the balance!"

CHAPTER XIII

Power

PETRA WAS a tall man like Solveg, but his features were less fine and he had a merrier twinkle in his eyes. When Asa and I called at his house, some hundred yards farther along the main street, he insisted that we should come in to meet his wife and two children and drink a cup of the delicious liquid which seemed to take the place of tea or coffee in Hesikos. Afterwards we took Janet and Spike away with us, while Petra said he would guide Professor Hermanoff to Solveg's house.

Asa led us through the city, stopping now and then to speak with friends and acquaintances. There was no sense of haste or hurry, and urgency appeared to be a word whose meaning was unknown in Hesikos.

Walking behind Janet and Asa, Spike and I listened with some surprise to their conversation.

"I do admire your tunic, Asa. What kind of material is it?"

"You'd call it silk, I believe. We have a little animal like your silk worm, which we breed on a special farm. All our clothes are made there."

"I'd love a piece to take back to Earth with me!"

"You shall have it, Janet. Just as much as you like. And before you leave I'll show you how we make a dress. We don't do any sewing, you know. We melt the edges of the stuff together, with a special iron."

"Yes—I noticed there were no seams in your dress. What a marvellous idea!"

With a mischievous smile Asa glanced back over her shoulder. "Don't you think Jeremy would look nice in a tunic like this?"

"Oh, he would!" Janet pretended to be serious. "We must see about making one for him."

"You jolly well won't!" I said. "A jersey and shorts are good enough for me!"

As the girls laughed, Spike patted my shoulder. "That's the spirit, bud! Fashions don't worry us, do they?"

Finally we came to an open space. Behind us lay the city. On the opposite side was a long, low-roofed building set against the living rock of the cavern's innermost wall. Asa told us that this was the power-house and remarked that Spike and I should probably be more interested in it than in dresses.

She pressed a switch and an iron door slid open. We were immediately conscious of a persistent humming noise, and as our eyes grew accustomed to the light we saw a great room lined with banks of switches and dials, with a number of small machines dotted about the stone floor. Spike said at once that it reminded him of the Central Power Station in Chicago and that even the clean metallic smell was the same.

At the back of the room was a much bigger machine surrounded by a railing. It was covered by a hood of black metal, but from one side there projected a flywheel spinning at speed.

"Is that the main dynamo?" Janet asked, as we went towards it.

Asa nodded. "You might call it the heart of Hesikos. It has never stopped running for thousands of years. If it did, we should all perish."

We stood by the railing and listened to its powerful whine, which rose and fell like the voice of a living creature.

"That's the sound we heard in the tunnel," I said. "Uncle Lachlan was sure it was a dynamo."

"You would hear it coming up through a ventilator shaft," returned Asa. "We have many shafts of that kind, connected with the power-house here, to keep the air of the city fresh." Suddenly she broke off as an elderly man with stiff brown hair came towards us across the floor. "But here is Dorman, our chief electrician," she said. "He will explain everything."

Dorman bowed to us. "You are our friends from Earth? I am glad you have come."

He was a different type from the other inhabitants of Hesikos. He wasn't quite so tall, and his shoulders were broader and more muscular. But, like the rest, his voice was gentle and kind.

"Janet and Jeremy and Spike want to inspect all your machinery," Asa told him.

"Of course," he answered. "But first of all let them come with me to the window—up there in the rock."

We followed him up a flight of worn stone steps to a platform. This was level with a thick sheet of transparent material set in the wall of rock. We looked through it and were astonished by what we saw. On the other side lay a dark tunnel, and through this tunnel there rushed a great volume of water, which sometimes leaped and splashed against the window.

"Why," exclaimed Janet, "it's a river! An underground river!"

"We can't hear it," said Spike. "Why is that?"

Dorman tapped the window. "This is solid mica—and soundproof like the iron door. The river drives the dynamo," he went on to explain, "which in turn charges the storage batteries—and from the batteries we distribute the electricity required for all our purposes; light and heat, and power for the various factory machines. Most important of all, power for the Electronome."

I said: "But when the ground up above is frozen during the winter, doesn't the river dry up?"

"No." Dorman smiled. "It comes from an underground spring and eventually enters the great sea which covers our southern hemisphere."

Janet shivered. "How cold and dark it looks! I should hate to fall in there. . . ."

Spike wanted to know what happened when the dynamo needed repair. "Don't you have to stop it?" he asked.

"It is never stopped," replied Dorman. "But in fact it is a twin. We can use one part while the other is stopped for maintenance and repair."

"I get you. Quite an idea!"

"But how was it built in the first place?" I said. "I mean—do you manufacture iron and steel in Hesikos?"

"Yes, indeed. There are mines below the city, and metal works not far from here. But you will

understand that in the power-house—and elsewhere
—few replacements are necessary, and the trade is
not a busy one. The oil for the bearings we collect
from a well above ground during the summer."

Spike sighed. "It's all a miracle sure enough. But
it hangs together!"

"Why shouldn't it?" laughed Asa. "Come," she
went on, "let's go back and see the dynamo at close
quarters. Dorman is very proud of it."

The chief electrician led us down the steps. "You
must understand that it has been in the care of my
family for generations," he said. "My eldest son will
succeed me when I grow old."

"Doesn't it worry you to have such a responsi-
bility?" Janet asked.

"No, we are trained to ignore anxiety. Otherwise,
as the life of Hesikos draws to a close, we should be
depressed and sad."

We crossed the floor and once again stood near the
dynamo. Dorman opened a small gate in the pro-
tective railing and we went close in beneath the
giant flywheel. Presently he touched a lever. As if
by magic the whine of the machine rose to a frenzied
pitch. The flywheel flashed round faster than the
eye could follow.

I looked at Dorman. His eyes were blazing with
love and enthusiasm, and I realised that to him this
great hulk of swirling metal was like a god.

"Listen!" he cried. "Listen to its power—and its
life!"

CHAPTER XIV

The Electronome

W<small>E STAYED</small> there for at least an hour, while
Dorman explained the power-system in detail.
Then Asa took us back through the city to a small
building with shining metal walls. It stood by itself
in a central square, removed by at least fifty yards
from all the other houses. As we approached it, I
had an odd feeling—as if there was danger in the
air.

While we were crossing the empty square Professor
Hermanoff appeared from a side street and joined
us. He was smiling and apparently in excellent
spirits.

"Solveg said I should find you here," he told us.

Asa took his arm. "You're just in time, Professor.
We're going to see the Electronome."

"How's the argument going?" I asked.

"Between Solveg and your uncle? Well—it is
friendly, but at the same time furious. I thought it
better that I should come away, because I do not
agree with either of them!"

Asa smiled. "It is something new for Father to
have an argument! It will do him good."

She pressed a switch in the wall of the isolated
building, and the door slid to one side. At first we
could see nothing, for the light inside was dim; but as

soon as we set foot across the threshold the feeling of danger became more acute. It was a tingling feeling, as if invisible hands were trying to touch us.

Then, at the far end of the apartment, we saw a red eye glowing on the wall and beneath it something that looked like a glass box with a tangle of wires inside. As we went towards this box, across the cool tiled floor, I judged that it was about ten feet long and three feet in height. It stood on a kind of trestle made from the same shining metal as the walls of the building—probably an iridonium alloy.

Spanning the whole width of the apartment was a railing which kept us several yards away from the instrument. Asa told us that its cover was of mica, and we stood watching it in fascinated silence. Every few seconds the wires inside pulsed red like transparent veins and we heard a delicate whirring sound. It came to me that this thing they called the Electronome must be alive, breathing there like a sleeping beast—tr-r-r-ick . . .tr-r-r-ick . . . tr-r-r-ick. . . .

It was Spike who broke the silence. "If the dynamo is the heart of Hesikos, then I guess this must be its brain?"

Asa nodded. "In a way—though, of course, the real brain of Hesikos exists in the thoughts of its people. The Electronome is only a receiver and transmitter of thoughts. That sound you hear comes from the scanning beam which constantly circles the universe."

"Those wires inside," said Janet, in a small voice, "they're like the cells of a living brain."

I made up my mind to defy its influence. "How does it work?" I asked, abruptly.

Asa glanced across at me. "You see the hand-grip terminals at the right-hand side? When the Electronome is adjusted to the proper wavelength, the operator holds these tightly. His thoughts are then magnified and transmitted by the machine; and presently, if conditions are favourable, he receives thoughts in return."

"It seems incredible," Janet put in. "Could *we* use it? I mean, those of us from Earth?"

"No. The operator must be a Hesikian, with the power in himself to transmit thoughts."

Hermanoff was leaning over the railing to get a better view. "It is a most wonderful invention," he said quietly. "Cannot we go closer?"

Asa shook her head. "That would be dangerous." And when Spike asked why, she pressed her fingers nervously together and went on: "It is difficult to explain. There is a power in the machine—a radiation of energy, if you like. It might kill anyone not trained to resist it."

"You mean the mind?" said Hermanoff, quickly. "You mean it might kill the mind—not the body?"

"Yes. Can't you feel—even from here—a kind of terror?"

Janet shivered. "I do. Just a little. . . ."

Asa smiled and put her arm round Janet's waist and said: "Oh, but I mustn't spoil your first day in our city! The power of the Electronome is there, but we can ignore it. Come away now. I should like to show you the school and the college, and our food factory."

Spike grinned, matching her light-heartedness.

"That ought to suit Jeremy—especially the food factory!"

I was glad to be out of the strange, quiet building; but for a long time, with the eyes and ears of imagination, I could see the pulsing red wires and hear the daunting sound: tr-r-r-ick . . . tr-r-r-ick . . . tr-r-r-ick.

As the afternoon went on, however, and we were introduced to teachers and professors, and to the men and women who made delicious food out of the fruit and plants, my uneasiness gave way to admiration for the people of Hesikos. They had reached a wonderful state of civilisation. Enmity and even argument were unknown, and each individual appeared anxious to help his neighbour if he could.

And yet all the time I felt that something was missing—I couldn't tell exactly what. Life on the lost planet was smooth and friendly and efficient; but it occurred to me that it was somehow tasteless, like an egg without salt.

That night Uncle Lachlan, Professor Hermanoff, Spike and I were given a small villa to ourselves. It stood on the opposite side of the street from Solveg's house, where Janet was going to sleep with Asa. We sat up late, discussing the experiences of the day and exchanging views on our astonishing discoveries; but eventually we became too sleepy for talk, and we retired to our bedrooms. Not long afterwards the lights of the city went out, and darkness fell about us like a blanket.

Spike and I shared a room at the front of the house, each of us having a bed made of the usual plaited fibre. It was so comfortable that I drowsed off almost at once.

Suddenly, however, I was wide awake again.

I heard Spike's quiet voice. "Jeremy—d'you reckon everyone's asleep?"

I glanced at the illuminated hands of my wrist watch. "I think so. It's nearly two hours since we came to bed."

He was silent for a time. Then he said: "If they're asleep, neither Solveg nor any of his people should be able to read our thoughts at this moment."

I asked him what was on his mind.

"I can't help thinking about that Electronome. I wish I could make a diagram of its wiring, to make experiments when we get back to Earth."

"But Asa said we'd be hurt if we went near it."

"I'm not so sure." There was scepticism in his voice. "Maybe she just *said* it was dangerous—to keep us from finding out its secrets."

"Janet felt something. And so did I."

"That could have been auto-suggestion. . . . You know, Jeremy, I've a good mind to take a torch and go and examine it now."

"Gosh—you wouldn't do that!"

"Why not? They don't think much of our intelligence here, but the Electronome is based on electricity, and we should be able to understand it."

"There's more to it than electricity, Spike. I was scared of it."

"That's nonsense! Why should anyone be scared of a machine?"

"I don't know. It—it's uncanny, somehow."

He laughed to himself. "Asa's got you the way

she wants us all to be! I don't believe it's dangerous—
and I'm going to see it now!"

I heard him getting up and putting on his shoes.
I was unwilling to leave my bed, but even more
unwilling to let Spike down.

"All right," I answered, swinging my feet on to
the floor, "if you're going so am I. You could never
make a diagram without having somebody to hold
the torch."

"Good for you, kid!" His voice was warm and
approving. "Come on, then. If we move quietly we
shouldn't disturb anyone."

"I don't like it," I said. "It's as if we weren't
trusting Asa and Solveg."

"Aw, boloney!" Without a sound he opened the
door to the street. "If we don't lose our way," he
whispered, "we should reach the central square in
about five minutes."

The city was as silent as a grave. As we went
quickly along the dark, deserted pavements, guided
by our torch, I had a feeling that if we even sneezed
the sound would rise up to the great dome above us
and come echoing back to waken everybody. We
walked on tip-toe, and not until we started to cross
the central square did we exchange a word.

As we approached the building with the shining
walls, I blurted out: "There doesn't seem to be a
soul awake!"

Spike chuckled. "No need for nightwatchmen
here. They haven't had criminals on Hesikos for
thousands of years."

"It's a queer place," I said. "Have you noticed
how they just ignore anything nasty or difficult?"

"Yeah. I agree with Dr. McKinnon. They're not *trying* any more. If a big disaster did happen, they'd pack in right away."

The beam of the torch picked out the switch beside the door. Spike pressed it, and the door opened with a kind of oily whisper. Inside the apartment the red light still shone above the Electronome, and in the dark the wires beneath the mica cover seemed to pulse and glow with additional power.

We padded across the tiles and stood with our hands on the railing.

"It—it looks *alive!*" I whispered.

"Be your age, Jeremy!"

But now there was a hint of uncertainty in his voice; and as we stood listening to the steady tr-r-r-ick of the instrument, I could feel him trembling a little.

"I hate that sound!" I said. "It seems to be mocking us—daring us to come closer!"

"Hooey!" he returned, sharply. "It's just a machine made out of mica and copper wire." Then he pulled himself together. "Well, no good wasting any more time. You take the torch, and stay here. I'll duck under the railing and try to make the diagram."

"All right. But take care, Spike."

"Don't worry. Here goes. . . ."

He straightened up beyond the railing. Then, within the beam of the torch, he began to walk towards the Electronome. As I watched, his step became slower and slower. And suddenly, a yard away from the machine, he stopped altogether.

H

There was something odd and unnatural about him.

"Spike," I cried, "why have you stopped? What's the matter?"

He didn't move, but his voice came to me, tight and muffled, like the voice of a suffocating man. "I—I don't know. There's something. . . . My mind's going blank, Jeremy. I can't think. . . ."

I stooped beneath the railing. "I'll help you, Spike."

"No!" he called out shrilly, as if hands were constricting his throat. "Keep back—there *is* a power in the machine!"

But I ignored the warning. I ignored the fear that churned inside me. Spike was my friend.

I reached him and put my arm about his shoulders. He leaned against me, muttering: "Jeremy—go back! Go back!" Then his knees began to buckle.

I tried to pull him away towards the railing, but to my horror I felt a numbness creeping through my body, like the numbness which follows a shot of cocaine at a dentist's. I couldn't think, either.

The torch dropped from my fingers. Spike slid out of my arms and collapsed like a dead man on the floor.

All I could see was the red pulsing wires inside the Electronome. All I could hear was the sound of its breathing: tr-r-r-ick . . . tr-r-r-ick . . . tr-r-r-ick. . . .

The red wires grew bigger and bigger. The sound began to roar like an approaching train. I struggled to escape, but there was no escape. And at last the wires exploded in my head with a searing flash, and the sound poured in and engulfed me in a terrible black silence.

CHAPTER XV

The Talking Bird

THE VOICE came to me as if from a vast distance. *"Jeremy! Come back, Jeremy!"*

"Leave me alone," I whispered. "I want to sleep."

"You must not sleep!" Again the voice, echoing down a long tunnel. *"Come back, Jeremy! Come back!"*

The command was so insistent that I couldn't ignore it. I moved weakly, and the numbness began to drain from my body.

"What is it? Why do you want me?"

"You must not sleep! Wake up, Jeremy—there is nothing to be afraid of now."

I struggled to obey. I seemed to be swimming in the smothering depths of a pool of silence. But now I could use my limbs. I was growing stronger. The will to live grew stronger, too. I struggled up and up until at last my head emerged from the pool and I drew in a great breath of intense relief. . . .

I sat up and saw Solveg bending over me, his bright eyes only a few inches from my own. "Where am I? What happened?" I said.

He put his hand on my shoulder and set me back against a pillow. "Now you are awake," he smiled. "That is good."

"But where am I?"

"Lie still, my son. You are in bed at my house.

We found you in the nick of time and brought you back."

Then I remembered. The Electronome—and Spike. "But Spike!" I exclaimed. "Is Spike all right?"

"Yes. He also has—wakened up. Janet and Asa and Professor Hermanoff are with him."

I turned and saw that Uncle Lachlan was standing on the other side of my bed. He looked across at Solveg. "How can I thank you?" he said. "I thought for a moment he would never come round." Then—in a kind of reaction, I think—he blazed at me: "What possessed you to do it, Jeremy? You were warned it was dangerous!"

"I know," I answered. "But Spike and I—we wanted to make a diagram of the wiring. We thought Asa was exaggerating."

His craggy jaw was set. "You had no right to abuse her hospitality! Had Solveg not been awake— had he not felt your terror in his own mind—you would both be dead by now."

Solveg made a gesture of restraint. "Let him be, my friend. He and Spike are young. They did not understand. If they made a mistake, they have been sufficiently punished. Let us forget it."

"You are very kind," replied my uncle.

I was bitterly ashamed and stammered out an apology. Then I added: "But—but can you tell me what actually happened?"

Our host laughed in his blond beard. "You see, Dr. McKinnon, even in sickness your nephew is still a scientist!"

"My nephew, I hope, has learned a valuable

lesson," said Uncle Lachlan, at his driest. "A lesson not to meddle in things he doesn't understand!"

"Of course he has." Solveg poured oil on troubled waters. "And at least he and Spike had courage. . . . Now, Jeremy," he went on, "I will try to explain what happened as simply as I can. The Electronome, which radiates our thoughts through space, is worked by electricity; but its main constituent is iridonium, the metal which you know about and which is found only in our planet. Charged with electricity, iridonium creates a field of radio-active power which paralyses an ordinary mind—a mind not trained to resist it. Had I not roused your uncle and Asa and gone to your rescue, you and Spike would have died. As it was, I had to recall the ancient art of reviving the mentally injured, and luckily my fingers were guided to the right veins in your head."

It was only later that I fully understood the fortunate escape we had had; but meanwhile I could appreciate quite well why Uncle Lachlan was so relieved, and so angry at the same time.

"You and Spike are lucky," he said. "Solveg tells me that there ought to be no ill effects whatsoever."

"None at all," agreed our host. "But they must both lie quietly for a time. Then Asa will bring them a meal and a reviving drink."

"Well, these are your orders, Jeremy. See that you carry them out. We have to leave you now. Solveg is going to show us some ancient books in his library."

I obeyed instructions. In fact, I was asleep when Asa came in with a tray of food. When she woke me

up she showed no signs of being annoyed by all the
trouble Spike and I were causing her. Instead she
seemed anxious that we should get better as soon as
possible.

"Try sipping the drink first," she said. "It's made
from what we call the Apples of Hesikos. You
tasted them before, I think, on your first expedition."

"Yes. They're like red pears turned upside down."

"There's a powder in the drink as well," she told
me. "A tonic powder which we get from the sap of
the tree."

I swallowed a sip or two, and it certainly made
me feel right on top of the world. Then I got busy on
the fruit cakes, while Asa watched with obvious
satisfaction. She explained that during the summer
the food producers went up into the daylight to pick
the fruit and gather in various kinds of wild corn.
The fruit was then preserved and the corn made into
flour for the cakes.

Finally, she said she must be off, as she had to
bring another tray to Spike.

"Is he all right?" I asked.

"Quite all right. Janet is keeping him company."

"Asa—before you go—I'm sorry that Spike and I
let you down about the Electronome."

She smiled. "Don't let it worry you, Jeremy. It
was curiosity—not really distrust. Here in Hesikos
we understand. . . . Now, I must go. When you get
up I'll take you to see where our birds and animals
live, in another cavern above us here."

That was one of the strangest sights in the underground city—the home of the birds and animals, I
mean.

Asa guided us along a narrow tunnel—Janet, Spike, Hermanoff and myself—and, after a walk of nearly five minutes, we emerged into a huge, brightly-lit chamber of rock carpeted with green turf. Here and there trees and flowers lifted their heads to the high roof.

The place was as fresh as a country glade, and the flowers gave off a wonderful perfume. At intervals along one wall I noticed the mouths of at least a dozen air-shafts. A small stream of clear cool water —probably piped in from the underground river— irrigated the ground and eventually disappeared again through a grid.

The cavern was filled with the chatter of brownies and the chirping of many birds. They sensed us at once and came crowding round, quite unafraid. I stooped down to touch one of the brownies, and somehow a lump came to my throat. He was so trusting, so friendly and happy. And yet he could not see us.

Some of the smaller birds perched on Asa's shoulders. She explained that the creatures of Hesikos lived here throughout the winter, in an atmosphere warmed by electricity. But in summer they often went outside to feed and drink.

Spike told her about the brownies we had seen two nights before, drinking at the river.

"Yes," she smiled. "They told us."

I stared at her. "You mean you understand their language?"

"Not the *sounds* they make, Jeremy. But they all have minds and thoughts of their own, and we can read their thoughts. The birds fly far and wide over the whole surface of Hesikos, and when the winter cold comes creeping down from the north they give us warning."

Janet spoke quietly. "But the poor little brownies, Asa—they're blind."

She nodded. "It happened when the climate changed. Before our ancestors rescued them from their underground burrows they had lost their sight. For centuries the scientists tried to give it back to them, but they couldn't."

"So," said Professor Hermanoff, "it was the animals that suffered most when the atomic bomb brought disaster to Hesikos?"

"I'm afraid it was. The birds can see, though."

A tiny bird on Asa's shoulder began to chirp excitedly, its beak almost in her ear. It had a red breast like a robin, and Hermanoff said it resembled the first bird he had seen outside the space ship.

Spike grinned. "I reckon it's wanting to tell you something!"

"I know she is!" said Asa. "This is Grenda, one of my favourites. . . . Come, Grenda, what is it?"

As the chirping became even more animated Asa smiled across at Hermanoff. "She's saying she *is* the bird you saw. She brought in the first news of summer."

"Well, what d'you know!" exclaimed Spike.

"She's trying to tell the Professor how grateful she is because he rescued her from the snow and warmed her in his hands."

"It is all most extraordinary," murmured Hermanoff. "But, of course, we on Earth understand very little about birds and animals. The facts of migration, for instance, they are quite beyond our powers of comprehension. But I suppose that some day we shall be able to read their thoughts as you do, and understand."

Grenda gave us another bout of chirping. It was comical to see all the other creatures grouped around, intent on listening.

Asa allowed her to finish. Then she explained: "She says she was flying over the river this morning— where the flood was—and she saw a strange object lying on the bank. You travelled down from the north in it, she says."

"She must mean the jeep," said Spike. "I wonder if it's badly damaged?"

"Grenda won't be able to tell you that," laughed Janet. "I don't suppose she's much of a mechanic."

Asa smiled. "She has no idea what a jeep *is*. There is only an impression in her mind of something unusual."

As the small bird flew off Spike said eagerly: "Asa—d'you think your engineers would be able to repair our jeep?"

"Oh, I'm sure they would. Before the cold came our ancestors built all kinds of vehicles—even electric trains which climbed the cliffs. We do not make machines like that today, of course, but our engineers retain the knowledge of how to construct and repair them. Tomorrow my father will send men out to recover your vehicle and make it move, if they can. . . . Come now, I will show you where the birds and animals store their food. The birds here in the ground, the animals over there among the tree trunks."

Later on she took us to join Solveg and Uncle Lachlan in the library, where we saw books and films preserved in transparent air-tight cases, which showed us life on the planet thousands of years ago. What struck me at once was how like the Earth today Hesikos had been. Only the print in the books was different. We couldn't make out a word, of course, but Asa translated it for us.

In those days, it seemed, each division of the people had spoken a different language, and there was much confusion. But when the survivors of the cold came to live in the underground city, they had developed the power of thought transference, and language became unimportant. As a result, the Hesikians had lost their suspicion and distrust of one another.

"And you gained goodwill, which benefited yourselves," said Uncle Lachlan. "But in my humble opinion—with the skill and knowledge at your disposal—you should have reached out and benefited the world as well."

"But we invented the Electronome," Solveg reminded him. "We used it to pacify the Earth ten thousand years ago—and to help you and your friends."

"Yes. And we are grateful. But there is so much more you could have done—and could still do—by building a new world here on Hesikos. Instead of that you have shrunk into yourselves and refuse to face up to your responsibilities. But where is your faith—your hope for the future?"

Solveg looked uneasy. "Dr. McKinnon," he said, "it is difficult for me to adjust my thoughts to yours. What you do not understand is that in a few years now, comparatively speaking, Hesikos will die."

"Why should it die?" My uncle barked out the question like a sergeant-major. "You have the scientific resources to make it live again."

"That may be so. But evil might come of unrestricted science. And then——"

Asa interrupted. "Father, why do you and Dr. McKinnon argue so much? Surely there are happier ways of spending our short time together?"

He looked gravely in her direction. "Yesterday I would have agreed with you, my daughter. But now —I do not know. My mind is troubled."

After a while Uncle Lachlan reminded Solveg that he was the only one who hadn't yet seen the dynamo.

"Ah, yes." Our host became more cheerful. "You must see the dynamo, my friend. In the meantime, Asa, will you take the others to our medical laboratory?"

"Of course, Father."

It seemed that in Hesikos penicillin and streptomycin were old and outdated remedies, and Janet, Hermanoff and Spike were looking forward to studying some of the wonderful new cures discovered by the Hesikians. But I chose to accompany Solveg and Uncle Lachlan. The great black dynamo fascinated me, and I wanted to see it again.

We separated, therefore, arranging to meet again for the mid-day meal at Solveg's house. About ten minutes later I was standing beneath the giant flywheel, listening to its powerful, challenging note, while Solveg and my uncle talked with the chief electrician.

"D'you mean to tell me, Dorman, that this dynamo never stops?"

"Never, Dr. McKinnon. If it did, we should know that the end of Hesikos had come. Without light and heat we could not live through the cold of even one winter."

"It is a beautiful machine. What are the brushes made of?"

"A special alloy—iron and iridonium," said Solveg.

Dorman opened a steel door in the cowling. "If you look inside, Dr. McKinnon, you will see the sparks of light as the brushes make contact with the revolving copper drums."

For a long time we remained there inspecting the machinery. At last, however, we said *au revoir* to Dorman. We were preparing to leave when there was a sudden muffled crash. The floor of the powerhouse trembled.

"What was that?" I exclaimed.

"I think it came from above ground," said Dorman. "There are often falls of rock after the melting of the ice and snow."

Then I saw his face change. The hum of the dynamo faltered. The flywheel began to spin slower and slower until finally it stopped altogether, leaving a desperate silence.

CHAPTER XVI

The Last Days of Hesikos

"Solveg, my dynamo! It has stopped!"

Dorman's anguished thoughts seemed to fill the silent power-house. His face had lost its expression of strength and confidence. Colour had drained from it, leaving it a muddy yellow.

Even Solveg himself appeared to be mentally and physically paralysed. "But that is impossible!" he said. "There is no flaw in the machinery."

It was Uncle Lachlan who pointed to a big dial on the wall, which showed the volume of water available to drive the dynamo. "Have you noticed? The pointer has gone back to zero."

"You are right," muttered Dorman. "But I do not understand."

Solveg pulled himself together. "That sound we heard. Something must have happened in the underground river that supplies the power."

The chief electrician ran towards the steps leading up to the soundproof window. I watched him cross the platform and peer through the transparent mica.

Meanwhile, Uncle Lachlan said: "But Solveg, surely it must be something quite simple? A breakdown of the driving-gear, perhaps?"

"That could not happen. Every part is in duplicate. If one piece of machinery breaks down its duplicate comes into action at once."

Dorman descended the steps again, slowly and with heavy feet. "It is the river!" he told us. "It has gone—dried up!"

"You mean there is no water left?" said my uncle, quickly.

"There is nothing at all, except slime and mud."

"Then it *was* that sound!"

Solveg agreed. "It must have been a fall of rock somewhere in the subterranean channel. That would change the course of the river. It has happened before in other places, but our engineers gave us no warning of this."

Dorman was gazing up at the motionless flywheel. His hands were clasped together against his chest, and there was pain in his eyes. "I—I cannot believe it!" he whispered. "This silence—this awful silence. . . . All my life I have worked here, tending the dynamo. Its sound became a part of me. Now there is nothing —nothing but silence. . . ."

"Dorman, that will do!" Uncle Lachlan spoke with sharp authority, and the chief electrician struggled to regain control of himself. "Tell me, for how long will the batteries supply light and heat without being recharged?"

"For two days and one night."

"Well, that gives you twenty-seven hours by our Earthly reckoning. Surely in that time you can find the obstruction and remove it."

"You do not understand. We have no means of removing it."

"What! Don't tell me you're giving in already?"

Solveg laid a gentle hand on my uncle's arm. "Dr. McKinnon, Dorman means that any obstruction which has stopped the river would require an explosive to break it up."

"Of course—I know that! But——"

"I have told you. For a hundred thousand years explosives have been outlawed on Hesikos. Even the formulae for their manufacture were destroyed."

I could see that Uncle Lachlan was taken aback by this. He frowned and slowly rubbed his chin with the back of his hand. "Yes—you did tell me. But there must be another method."

"There is none." Solveg spoke with infinite patience. "This is the end of our planet, my friend— the end of life on Hesikos. We have been waiting for this moment for many years. Dorman here—he is dismayed and sad because the dynamo is silent, but like the remainder of my people he is not afraid."

The chief electrician looked away from his machine and nodded. "I am not afraid. My mind has been trained to meet this final disaster."

Uncle Lachlan's face was flushed. "Final disaster!" he exclaimed. "Oh, you make me mad! There *is* no final disaster. There's always a way out."

"Please," said Solveg, "please do not excite yourself on our behalf. You must look after yourselves and leave us as soon as possible. My engineers will find and repair your vehicle——"

"Never mind our vehicle! Think of your own predicament. Evil has come to Hesikos. Face it! Defeat it!"

"But there is nothing we can do. It is fore-ordained."

"How foolish! Nothing is fore-ordained! We have the freedom of our own minds and wills!"

"Dr. McKinnon, I must ask you to be patient."

"Patient—tcha!" This was again the quick and irritable man I had known weeks ago at Inverard. Abruptly he went on: "You refuse to think of yourselves. Very well then, think of others. You possess wisdom and knowledge that will benefit the whole universe. Why should you be prepared to die and let all that wisdom and knowledge die with you?"

Solveg, in spite of himself, appeared to be impressed. "I—I see what you mean, Dr. McKinnon. But that is not our philosophy."

Uncle Lachlan used restraint. "In my opinion," he said, "your philosophy is a barren stick!"

"I cannot agree. We have evolved our philosophy through the centuries. Now that the test has come you will realise how valuable it is."

"Oh, it's valuable all right! As valuable as the desert sand for a frightened ostrich!" My uncle glared at him. Then he shrugged his shoulders. "But it seems that anything I say makes no difference. What are you going to do now?"

"I will use the Electronome," said Solveg, "to tell my people the truth and prepare them for what is going to happen." He turned to the chief electrician. "You will stay here, Dorman, and regulate what remains of the electricity. Dr. McKinnon, you and Jeremy will go back to my house, as arranged. There, with the others, you will hear my thoughts as I send them to my people."

"Tcha!" Uncle Lachlan moved away, angrily.

"With all your science and skill, that it should come to this!"

We gathered in Solveg's house—Janet and Asa, Professor Hermanoff and Spike, Uncle Lachlan and myself. And as we waited the power came to us. We could almost *hear* Solveg's voice: "*The moment has come—the moment for which our minds have been prepared. The river is blocked, and even now life is draining from the city. In two days all light and heat will be gone. Thereafter we must wait with resignation for the end, in the cold of winter. Until that time let peace and charity be amongst us.*"

I was watching Uncle Lachlan's face. I don't think I have ever seen it so stern and angry. . . .

That afternoon engineers went out and came back to report that our jeep had been repaired and was ready at the entrance to the tunnel. There was a strange quiet in the city, like the quiet before a thunderstorm, but the atmosphere remained warm and pleasant, and a glow of light still shone down from the silvery vault of the cavern.

Towards evening I was with Janet and Professor Hermanoff and Uncle Lachlan—in Solveg's house— when suddenly Spike came in. His clothes were covered with mud and slime, and there was excitement in his eyes.

"Dr. McKinnon," he said, "I did as you told me. I got through the window when Dorman wasn't looking and crawled along a ledge above the channel of the underground river."

"Go on."

"The obstruction is about four hundred yards along the tunnel—a mass of solid rock dislodged from the roof. The river is piled up behind it and is

I

being directed into another channel well above its previous level."

Janet said: "Then there's no chance that the river will break through again, on its own?"

"Not a hope."

"Where do you think the water is going now?" asked Hermanoff.

"Into another channel altogether, nowhere near this place. I reckon Solveg was right. There's only one answer—blow up the fallen rock and let the river come through as it did before."

Uncle Lachlan rubbed his chin. "How much gelignite would be required for that?"

"Well, for a thorough job—fully guaranteed—I guess you'd need up to ten pounds."

"We've got the twenty sticks you rescued from the jeep—roughly five pounds. Any good?"

"Could be, Doctor. But no guarantee. We can't bore a proper hole in the rock, that's the trouble."

"So this is what you've been planning," said Janet, quietly. "To blow up the obstruction and save the city, in spite of what Solveg says?"

Uncle Lachlan nodded. "Spike and I will take the gelignite now and try to destroy the rock."

"But, Lachlan, the risk!" Hermanoff was distressed. "You may be trapped in there!"

"We must do *something*," replied my uncle, irritably. "This fatalism—this soft resignation—I will have no part in it! Solveg and his people have many things to teach us. But we have something to teach them as well. There is no progress without risk. Without sacrifice, if need be."

"Is there no other way?" asked Janet.

"None that I can see."

Spike butted in: "By the way, I discovered something else. The big rock in the channel is lying hard up against the walls. For the maximum effect the charge will have to be set inside the narrow crevice below it. You and I, Dr. McKinnon, we're too big to get in there."

The room became silent. Outside there was uneasy movement in the streets. Solveg and Asa were visiting the leaders of the city, making arrangements for the last days of Hesikos.

Then suddenly I knew the answer. "Spike," I said, "I'm a bit slimmer than both of you. Could I get into that crevice?"

He looked me in the eye. Quietly he said: "I guess you could, Jeremy."

"In that case I'll go with you instead of Uncle Lachlan."

Janet and Hermanoff protested at once, but I let the arguments about my age and inexperience flow past me. For a time Uncle Lachlan didn't say a word. He kept staring at the tiled floor, and I couldn't help wondering what was in his mind.

At last he said: "Do you understand the risk you'd take?"

I told him I did.

"Do you understand that you and Spike might never come back?"

"Yes."

"Tell me, what is your reason for wanting to do this?"

"*You* wanted to do it. And I agree with what you say about facing up to things."

He smiled, and his face lost all its cragginess. "Thank you, Jeremy," he said.

Presently he turned to Spike. "I think that settles it. We'll speak to Solveg before you go and explain our plan to him."

CHAPTER XVII

Dark Silence

W‌E FOUND Solveg in the power-house, standing by the battery controls. He was relieving Dorman, who, for a short spell, had gone home to his family.

Uncle Lachlan told him what Spike and I intended to do. He listened gravely. Then he said: "I do not wish them to do it."

My uncle stuck out his chin. "Why, may I ask?"

"Explosives are evil. No good can come out of evil."

"I have told you before, Solveg, we people from the Earth do not agree with that philosophy. Spike and Jeremy are going now, whether you wish it or not."

"My friend, my friend, why do you insist? We did not ask your help."

"But can't you see?" Uncle Lachlan's arms went out in a gesture of annoyance. "If Spike and Jeremy succeed you may be encouraged to create a new way of life on Hesikos—to devote your powers to teaching other worlds."

"That may be so. But if they fail——"

"If they fail, the position will be no worse that it is now."

"I still do not wish them to go."

For a moment Uncle Lachlan was silent. A pulse

throbbed beneath the iron-grey hair on his left temple, and I saw his fingers clench.

"Do you think I am glad that they are going?" he exclaimed at last, his voice trembling. "Spike my friend—and Jeremy my own nephew! Do you realise that they are prepared to sacrifice their lives for you and your people?"

Solveg's expression changed. He laid his hand on my uncle's shoulder. "I am sorry, Dr. McKinnon. There is that side of it to be considered."

"Very well." Uncle Lachlan reverted to his normal manner. Then abruptly he turned away. "Are you ready, Spike?" he asked.

"Yeah."

"You, Jeremy?"

"Yes."

"You have the torch and the gelignite?"

"We're all set," said Spike.

"Then good luck and—*au revoir*."

We climbed the steps and opened the mica window.

Inside the subterranean channel it was cold and damp, and the rocky walls seemed to whisper as we moved. It was a ghostly place, filled with vague dangers which I didn't try to define.

At first we walked along the floor. The vanishing river had left behind it a thin layer of mud. Before we had gone a hundred yards our shoes were sodden and I, for one, had begun to feel shivery and uncomfortable. Soon I found it an effort even to lift my feet.

Spike flashed the torch on the walls and the high roof. "Fifty yards ahead we'll be able to climb up on to the ledge I told you about. It takes us all the way to the obstruction."

After a time I said: "Kind of eerie, this place."

"Sure is," he answered, lightly. "Know what it reminds me of?"

"What, Spike?"

"One of the big sewage pipes beneath Chicago. When I was a student we were taken down one day to be shown how the system worked. They'd shut off the water, of course, but I was scared stiff in case anyone would turn it on by mistake."

I understood exactly what he meant. At the back of my mind was the idea that the water might after all break through and come rushing and thundering towards us out of the dark.

Then I thought of something else. "When I crawl into the crevice under the rock," I said, "and you put a match to the fuse, what happens next? I mean, will we have time to get back to the power-house before the explosion?"

"Yeah, I think so. This fuse"—he touched the coil of white stringy material which he carried on his left shoulder—"I made it out of what Asa calls 'wool'. It's about twenty feet long and should take twenty minutes to burn. That ought to give us time to get away."

Presently the beam of the torch picked out a dark ledge above our heads. There were several footholds in the wall below, and Spike climbed it without difficulty. I followed him, not so easily, but he leaned down and got a hold beneath my right arm-pit and helped me scramble up over the edge.

There wasn't much room between the ledge and

the roof of the tunnel—only about two and a half feet, I should say. As we began to crawl along the smooth and comparatively dry stone surface, we had to keep our heads down, otherwise we might have been knocked out by protruding parts of the roof. Spike led the way, while I came closely at his heels.

I couldn't help being scared. The suggestion of whispering remained in the dark silence; and every yard we moved the closed-in feeling grew stronger in my mind. My knees were scarred and bruised by contact with the rock, but at the time I scarcely noticed.

To keep my courage up I started to talk. "Spike," I said, "remember when you took the gelignite from the jeep you thought you'd made a mistake? It was lucky you did."

"Yeah. Queer how things turn out." He pulled himself along quickly, and it seemed to me that he understood exactly how I felt and was doing his best to keep the conversation going. "My father always hated to get rid of anything. His study was piled with junk—screwdrivers, photos, old newspapers, ginger-jars. He said if you keep a thing long enough you always find a use for it."

I began to feel better. "Pity the people of Hesikos didn't keep their knowledge of explosives."

"Yeah. It would have been easier for us today, kid!"

As we crawled along, chatting aimlessly, the whispering grew louder and deeper, until at last it was a muffled rumble which echoed dully along the ledge.

"What's that noise?" I blurted out.

"I guess it comes from beyond the fallen rock. Loose boulders, I'd say, rolling along the bed of the river. We're getting quite close now."

Later on I said: "Spike, what if the explosion brings down more of the roof?"

He grinned back over his shoulder. "Well, I reckon that's one of the risks your uncle talked about."

Soon afterwards he stopped. The torch-beam played on a mass of stone which fitted closely against the wall of the tunnel. Its surface was wet and slimy, and at its edges small amounts of water trickled down.

He tapped with the butt of the torch. "This is it," he said, cheerfully. "There's thousands of tons of water piled up through there—just twenty feet away. If you listen you can hear it spilling off into another channel."

Above the beating of my heart I could distinguish a sibilant rushing sound, punctuated by the rumble of slowly moving boulders. But Spike had already started to climb down to the floor of the tunnel.

The wall was more slippery here. As a matter of fact, I lost my grip half-way down and fell about ten feet. Spike steadied me as I landed, however, and no harm was done.

Here the floor was inches deep in liquid mud. In the torchlight I saw the great rock jammed tight in the tunnel, and Spike showed me the space underneath into which I had to crawl. This was only about eighteen inches high. I could understand that if the gelignite were tamped in there, directly underneath the rock, the explosion would be much more likely to be effective than if it were set off against its side.

"Better get cracking," said Spike.

I nodded and took the torch.

"Sing out when you get stuck. Then I'll push the gelignite in after you."

"Okay."

I went down on my stomach among the mud. I didn't say anything to Spike, of course, but I couldn't help imagining what would happen if the great rock suddenly sank down on top of me.

It was a tight squeeze, but though all my instincts were against it I kept wriggling farther and farther in. The rock above seemed to get heavier and heavier on my back. An hysterical idea occurred to me. I was Atlas, with the whole world on my shoulders. Just in time I prevented myself from shouting with laughter.

Then I found that I had reached the end of the crevice. In front of me was solid rock. I forced myself to shout back the information to Spike.

His voice came to me, muffled but somehow comforting. "Fair enough. Stand by for the gelignite. I'll push it in the full length of my arm. You ought to be able to reach it."

Lying parallel with the narrow wall of rock I stretched my left arm back. I could hear Spike breathing heavily as he manoeuvred himself in as far as possible, and presently my groping hand touched the bag of gelignite.

"Twenty sticks, Jeremy. Got 'em?"

"Yes, I've got them."

I pulled the bag towards me. Fumbling in the wet, cramped darkness I took out the sticks and tamped them end to end against the rock with loose stones and mud. I had put the last of them in position when there was a sudden thudding noise, and the whole rock shook. I closed my eyes in abject terror.

Spike's voice came to me again. "Stick it, kid! That was just another loose boulder rolling up against the rock."

For a moment I couldn't answer. I felt that I was trapped, and a scream bubbled in my throat.

"Stick it out, Jeremy! Just another few seconds. . . ."

I fought hard to subdue the sick panic that had come over me, and I soon regained control.

"All right, Spike. . . . Give me the end of the fuse now."

He thrust it in. I caught it and tied it to one of the sticks of gelignite.

"How's it going?"

"Finished," I told him. "The fuse is attached."

"Great! Now get out of it—quick!"

I didn't need to be told. I squirmed and pushed desperately, and though the crevice was only about ten or twelve feet in length, it seemed to be a long time before I struggled clear and lay panting beside Spike in the open tunnel.

He gripped my shoulder. "You're a chip off the old block, kid! Tough as they come. . . ."

That helped me, and I got up on my knees. While I held the torch he took a box of matches from his pocket. He struck one, and the flare showed the thin line of white "wool" disappearing into the crevice. He put the flame to the "wool", and I saw it catch and begin to burn.

After a moment I glanced at Spike's face. Suddenly it had become lined and tense.

He jumped to his feet. "Come on, kid! It's burning faster than I thought. We'll have to move to get back to the power-house in time. . . ."

CHAPTER XVIII

The Roaring Torrent

WE SCRAMBLED up on to the ledge and began to crawl back in the direction of the power-house.

It was like a nightmare. We tried to move fast, but somehow we felt that we could never move fast enough. In my mind's eye I saw the burning fuse, its small smouldering flame creeping in beneath the rock towards the sticks of gelignite. It was only twenty feet long, I remembered, and I couldn't help thinking that the flame would reach the gelignite long before we had covered four hundred yards.

All the time, as we hurried along the ledge, there was a prickle of terror in my back. Every second I expected to hear the thunder of the explosion and the roar of the pent-up waters leaping after us. But the tunnel remained quiet, except for the whispering, thudding sounds which echoed along the ledge.

I was in a filthy state, plastered with mud from head to toe, and my knees and hands were bleeding from contact with the rock.

Spike came immediately behind me. He knew how desperately afraid I was and tried to encourage me. He kept saying that once we reached the end of the ledge we shouldn't have far to go.

I said something about the fuse burning faster than he had expected.

"Yeah," he answered. "I should have tested the rate of combustion more thoroughly, but I hadn't time. . . . Go on, Jeremy. Quicker if you can."

"It—it's so closed in here," I blurted out. "If the rock is destroyed and the water comes through——"

"Steady, kid—steady! Just concentrate on moving fast."

I did my best to obey. We were now nearly at the end of the ledge. When we reached it we should have to race through the clogging mud at the bottom of the channel. That would be the worst experience of all.

A current of air blew suddenly on my neck. Spike flicked up his torch, and we saw a narrow air-shaft above us. It was like the one from the power-house to the entrance tunnel and might indeed be a branch leading down from it.

Then we came to the end of the ledge. As I prepared to climb down I said: "Do you think we've time to reach the power-house?"

Spike answered sharply. "I don't know, Jeremy. I just don't know. It'll be a near thing——"

His words were cut off by a terrific explosion. Echoes reverberated through the tunnel, and the whole world seemed to be trembling. A blast of air swept past and nearly sucked us off the ledge.

"That's it!" I shouted.

"Yeah. Wait! Wait here on the ledge."

"Has the rock gone? D'you think the water's coming through?"

"Hold your horses! Listen. . . ."

In the distance there was a grumbling, splashing noise, as if angry giants were fighting waist-deep in water. It was a desperate moment as we crouched there in the dark waiting to see if the river would come through and overwhelm us.

．　．　．

They had gathered beside the dynamo—Solveg and Asa, Janet and Hermanoff, my uncle and Dorman. As the crash echoed through the open window, Professor Hermanoff was first to speak.

"Surely it cannot be the explosion already?"

"It *must* be," said Uncle Lachlan, grimly.

"But it is five minutes too soon."

That was the thought uppermost in all their minds. There had been a miscalculation. If the river came through Spike and I should be trapped and drowned. Janet began to cry, and Asa took her in her arms and tried to comfort her.

Solveg went across to Uncle Lachlan. "Perhaps the explosion has failed," he said. "Perhaps after all the river will *not* come through, and your friends will be safe."

My uncle stood as still as a rock. "That is a possibility," he replied in a flat voice. "But in any case we shall know quite soon. If the water reverts to its original channel, then the dynamo will start up again. Isn't that so, Dorman?"

"That is so, Dr. McKinnon."

Janet cried out: "But if the dynamo starts we'll know that Jeremy and Spike are dead!"

Asa held her closer. "Please, Janet," she said, quickly, "they may be safe."

My uncle remained motionless and tense. "Hermanoff," he said, "provided the explosion was successful, how long did we calculate it would take for the river to come through and start the dynamo?"

"Fifty seconds, Lachlan." The Professor looked at his watch. "That is, in about twenty seconds from now."

The power-house was very quiet. Janet dried her eyes and began to watch the flywheel above her head. It seemed utterly lifeless.

No one spoke until Hermanoff, again looking at his watch, began to mutter to himself: "Six . . . five . . . four . . . three . . . two . . . one. . . ."

Janet's hands flew to her throat. The flywheel moved—slowly at first then faster and faster. The hum of the dynamo grew in volume until at last it filled the power-house.

Dorman ran up the steps and looked through the window. "The river is rushing past!" he called to them. "Exactly as it did before!"

Lights above the dials glowed red. Pointers moved round, showing that the batteries were charging again and putting out a full load of electricity.

Uncle Lachlan's face was grey and craggy. "Hesikos is saved," he said to Solveg. "Spike and Jeremy have saved it."

Solveg bowed his head. "But our salvation has come at a terrible price."

Asa, however, refused to give up hope. "Spike and Jeremy may still be safe," she told her father. "I cannot feel in my mind that they are dead."

"That may be so," he answered, putting a hand to his forehead. "My power of reading distant thoughts has deserted me. This shock—this moment of triumph and disaster——"

"I have a plan to save them," she went on. "A plan that I must carry out alone."

He looked up in sudden dismay. "Does that mean you will risk your life?"

"Perhaps."

"But my daughter, you cannot do it! I——"

"Father, please understand! Spike and Jeremy risked their lives for us. I must risk mine for them. No good can come out of doing nothing."

He stared at her. In that moment all the teaching of his ancestors was being set aside for a new philosophy.

But at last, a tired and beaten man, he nodded: "Very well, Asa. You are young—and the future of Hesikos may now belong to the young. . . . Go, my daughter. Do what you intend to do."

Asa hurried away. . . .

After the explosion Spike and I remained crouched on the ledge, waiting; and in a matter of seconds we knew the answer. The grumbling, splashing sounds began to change, and soon there was nothing but a continuous roar—the roar of a great torrent of water coming towards us through the tunnel.

"We've done it!" shouted Spike.

"I know. But we're trapped!" I shouted back. "We'll never reach the power-house now! Even here on the ledge we're not safe. . . ."

He turned and began to scramble back the way we had come. "That air-shaft!" he yelled to me. "Maybe we can climb up into it."

K

The shaft was only a few feet away. In the light of his torch we saw rough footholds.

"Go on, kid! up you go!"

The torrent was nearly on us. I scrambled up, clinging for dear life to the rough edges of the rock. Spike came after me. So close was he that my foot struck his head. But he said nothing, for just then the river came plunging and crashing past below us.

I wedged myself inside the shaft. The water splashed across its mouth, and I realised that if we had remained on the ledge we should both have been drowned.

But what was our next move? We were like flies, poised precariously above the flood, and there seemed little chance that it would subside.

Spike shone his torch. The footholds continued on above our heads, finally disappearing round a bend in the shaft. "Climb!" he shouted. "Climb!"

I did as he told me, my muscles aching, my finger-nails torn and bleeding, the thought always at the back of my mind that if I slipped I should dislodge him and we'd both go hurtling down.

Slowly and painfully we moved higher and higher, below us the hungry river, above us we didn't know what. But at last we reached the bend and to our relief discovered that the place widened out to a kind of platform where we could rest. It seemed, however, that we were stuck there. Above our heads were two other separate shafts, but they were both perpendicular and looked unclimbable.

For a time we lay flat on the hard stone, recovering our nerves and our breath. The sound of the river was less insistent, but it remained as a menacing background to all our thoughts. We were safe enough for the present, but had we not perhaps escaped sudden death only to face a lingering agony which would be far more terrible?

At last I looked up and said: "Spike—where do you think those shafts lead to?"

"At a guess I'd say the one goes straight up to the entrance tunnel—the one you and your uncle discovered. The other may lead to where the birds and animals are. But possibly I'm wrong. The whole place must be honeycombed, otherwise the city—and this underground channel—wouldn't be so fresh."

"Any chance of climbing up into them?"

"I guess not, Jeremy."

"Then—then what's going to happen to us?"

He put an arm across my shoulders. "Hold it, kid! No need to panic yet. Solveg and Asa are bound to know that if we're alive at all we're here on this platform. They'll do something to help us, or I'm mistaken."

For what seemed like hours we lay there on the damp rock. Sometimes we talked. Sometimes we fell into an uneasy sleep, with the sound of the river in our ears. It became very cold.

I began to wonder what it would be like to die. Should we lose consciousness first, or should we *know* when it was going to happen? I wanted to scream, but I thrust my face against the stone and fought against it.

And then, quite suddenly, I wasn't afraid any more. In the light of the torch I saw that Spike was no longer anxious.

He glanced at his wrist watch. "Half an hour

we've been here," he remarked. "That's really not long."

"I don't suppose it is," I said, sitting up.

He grinned at me. "Queer thing, Jeremy. For the past few minutes it's Madge and Professor Bergman I've been thinking about. I wonder how they're getting on in the ship?"

"Maybe it's a good thing they don't realise what's happened to us."

He nodded. "Lucky the jeep's been fixed," he went on. "If we get out of here we'll be able to reach the ship again in about three days."

"Gosh, Spike—think of the story we'll take back to Earth! About the dynamo and the Electronome, about the people of Hesikos and how they can read our thoughts. . . ."

He patted my back. "That's better, kid. Now you're more like yourself."

Almost as he spoke we heard a sound above us, like the scrape of a shoe. Quickly we got to our feet.

The sound occurred again, nearer this time, and we knew that it was coming from the left-hand shaft. Something—or somebody—was coming down.

Then came the voice: "Spike, Jeremy—are you there?"

It was Asa, her words echoing dully in the confined space.

"Yes, we're here!" I yelled. "Safe and sound."

"That's wonderful. I'm on a ledge up here, but I've got a long rope, and I'll be with you in a moment. Then we'll all be able to climb back up. . . . Look out—I'm going to throw the end of the rope."

It thudded at our feet. Next moment Asa's legs

appeared. Then she was beside us on the platform, smiling as she caught our hands. She was happy to see us, but not so happy as we were to see her.

"How did you get here?" asked Spike.

"Down through the maze of shafts from the place where the birds and animals live. The other end of the rope is tied to the trunk of a tree up there."

"Gosh," I said, "you took a risk!"

"It was worth it, Jeremy. . . . Now, come on. It's going to be a long climb back, so we'd better not waste time."

CHAPTER XIX

Journey Home

IT WAS a difficult and tedious climb through the complicated system of air-shafts, but at last we found ourselves safe, with the birds and animals crowding round as we emerged into their beautiful cavern.

I was so thankful for our escape that the details of what happened afterwards are hazy in my mind. I know that Janet kissed me and that Uncle Lachlan kept me beside him for the rest of the day.

In the afternoon people gathered in the central square to thank us for having saved their lives. It was all very embarrassing. Children swarmed round Spike and me. They seemed to think we were heroes. Spike was one all right. But if they'd only known how scared I was in the tunnel. . . .

Solveg asked Uncle Lachlan to give his thoughts to the crowd, and—very unwillingly, I think—he spoke to them in his dry yet somehow brilliant way.

"My friends," he said, "we are Earth men, and our knowledge of science—and of goodness—is pathetically small compared with yours. And yet, maybe we have taught you something. Long ago you put aside your knowledge of explosives and atomic power, because you imagined that they were evil and no good could come of them. But Spike Stranahan and my—my nephew Jeremy have proved that you are wrong, that without moral and physical courage there can be no progress, not even in the planets and the stars. We are about to return to Earth, but one day soon we shall bring back to you the lost secrets of atomic energy. In your wise and good hands it ought to save Hesikos from extinction and create a new and vigorous life for this planet. In return we would ask you to use your influence upon *us*—upon our uneasy, divided but intensely vital world— your influence of charity and good will. . . ."

Shortly before we were due to leave—in fact, Janet and Spike had already gone to the entrance tunnel to pack the jeep—my uncle and Hermanoff and I were talking to Solveg in his house, when suddenly Asa came into the room. I saw at once that she had something serious to say, and I have an idea that Solveg knew what it was before we did.

"Father"—she rested her hand on his arm—"I should like to go with our friends to Earth."

"You mean now?" he said, quietly.

"Yes. Dr. McKinnon says there is evil on the Earth which we in Hesikos can cure. And before we can do that we must know about it."

"But my daughter——"

"Father, I have another reason. Some day I shall rule Hesikos in your place. If I have experience of another world and its problems my task here will be much simpler."

There was hurt in Solveg's eyes. But I saw pride in them, too.

"She is right," said Uncle Lachlan. "Let her come with us—even if only for a short time."

Hermanoff put in a word. "I agree with my colleague. And I also have a suggestion to make. While Asa visits Earth, I should like to remain here, learning and teaching."

For a moment no one spoke. I was amazed by the change that had come about in this man whose words had been so harsh and bitter on our first acquaintance.

Then Uncle Lachlan said: "Hermanoff, do you mean it?"

He smiled. "Of course, Lachlan. I can teach the scientists of Hesikos the theory of atomic energy, so that when you return they will readily absorb the practical details."

"But your country! Your country expects you back."

"Countries do not matter. Before I made my first journey into space I read a book. The author said something like this. 'Tribal conflicts and narrow-minded nationalism—how can they survive when men have seen the Earth as a pale crescent dwindling against the stars.' I did not fully understand what he meant until now. If Solveg and his people shall have me, I will stay in Hesikos."

And so it was arranged. Asa said good-bye to her father, and for three days and nights we travelled in the jeep through the pale green countryside of Hesikos, with the scent of the little white flowers always with us. Spike drove fast, with Uncle Lachlan beside him picking out the route, and Janet and Asa and I in the back.

At first we followed the course of the river which ran past the pointed hill. The water had now subsided to the merest trickle. Then we came to the great cliff, and Spike took us down safely along the narrow track.

On the morning of the fourth day we spotted the ugly red space ship in the distance, and a few hours later we had joined Madge and Professor Bergman again and Madge was offering Asa her first cooked meal. It was a steak and kidney pie, and I couldn't help smiling as Madge coaxed our guest to eat it.

"Come on, ducks," she said. "You'll enjoy it."

"It looks—strange somehow."

"Never mind 'ow it looks. It's the taste that counts."

And Asa really did enjoy it. Spike, however, told her that she was lucky. Miss Smith, he said, happened to be the best cook on Earth.

Madge giggled. "Get away with you, Mr. Stranahan! Pay no 'eed to 'im, Miss Asa. 'E and Jeremy pull my leg something cruel!"

"It's because they're both in love with you," said Janet.

"Oh, you're just as bad! But I will admit this— it's lovely to see you all back."

Asa finished her steak and kidney. "You know," she said, "I cannot understand why you are all so happy, with the danger of a journey to the Earth just a few hours away. Can you explain, Dr. McKinnon?"

"Well"—Uncle Lachlan rubbed his chin—"the reasons are complicated. For one thing, Hesikos has always had a happy influence on us. For another, we are looking forward to returning to our own people and telling them the story of the lost planet.

And last but not least—when you come to study us on Earth you'll find that we react to danger in a peculiar way. Danger stimulates us, and even though we are a little afraid we are inclined to enjoy it."

"Cor, lumme—speak for yourself!" Madge put in.

My uncle laughed. "Anyway, we're used to space voyages now, Asa. For most of us this will be the fourth take-off. Once you get used to a thing it always *seems* less dangerous. . . . By the way, Spike," he added, "have you checked the ship?"

"Yeah. She's wonderful. Andrieff certainly knew his stuff."

"While you were away," said Professor Bergman, "Madge and I repacked the parachute and filled the fuel tank with water. We are ready to take off at any time."

"Well done, Lars." My uncle got up from the table and glanced at his watch. "I think we should fix zero hour for tomorrow morning at six o'clock. That ought to ensure we land at Inverard about mid-day, two days from now."

"To be exact at thirty-nine minutes, twenty-seven seconds past twelve."

"Quite so. That leaves us ten hours in which to get ready and make everything ship-shape. I'm afraid with so many of us on board we shall have to leave the jeep behind, but that can't be helped. I told your father, Asa, to send someone for it. Your people can use it as a prototype for the new vehicles they are going to build."

There was a strange look in her eyes. "Hesikos will have changed when I come back," she said.

We took off at six o'clock the next morning, as Uncle Lachlan had planned. As the ship lifted under the tremendous urge of the jets I could see that Asa was scared, and she took some time to recover from the black-out. But she joined in the laughter when Janet remarked that it was the first time I hadn't been the last to come round.

"Well," I said, "it's kind of encouraging not to be 'tail-end Charlie' for once. But I was just thinking—Asa can't go about on Earth with that tunic and shorts. Specially in Scotland. She'd die of cold."

"Don't worry," replied Janet, unbuckling her safety-belt. "She and I are going to be dressmakers for the rest of the voyage. Aren't we, Asa?"

"Oh, yes. We've taken some cloth, Jeremy, and Janet is making me a jacket and slacks like she wears herself."

"M'm. Well, you're lucky having something to do, you two. Fifty-four hours is going to take a long time passing. I'm not so bad. I'm helping with the radar and the charts."

The hours went by, and the radar-screens went blank for a time as we sped through outer space at eighty miles per minute. But nothing happened at all, except that once, when we were about a hundred thousand miles from Earth and Professor Bergman and I were keeping watch while the others slept, we heard a curious singing noise. Obviously it came from outer space; but it soon passed, like a distant station fading out on the radio.

"What was it?" I said, rather nervously.

He shook his head. "I have no idea, Jeremy. It

may have been caused by the ship passing through a cloud of tenuous gas. I do not know."

"Could it have something to do with cosmic rays?"

"Perhaps. We have much to learn on the subject of outer space. But you know, I cannot help thinking of a phrase used by the French writer Montaigne. He talks of 'the music of the spheres'."

At twelve twenty next morning the flashes on the radar-screen were occurring once every two seconds. Uncle Lachlan came across and looked at my chart.

"Just two thousand miles to go," he said. "We ought to land exactly according to schedule." Then he stretched his arms and sighed a little. "Well, Jeremy, I shan't be sorry to see Inverard again. There was a time on Hesikos when I thought I never should."

"That was when you were alone, during the winter?"

"Yes. I used to sit in the ship—cold as ice even with the heaters on—and try to remember what Inverard was like. The heather on the hills, and the sunlight, and the green trees in the glen, and the quiet little burn running through. It helped to keep me alive."

"It must have been pretty awful! I wonder if Asa will think about Hesikos in the same way?"

"I expect she will, to a certain extent. But remember that her mind has been trained differently from ours. She won't allow sentiment to interfere with logic as much as we do. In any case, she and Janet have become very good friends."

At twelve twenty-five we fastened on our safety-belts. Uncle Lachlan looked at his watch. First he released the parachute in the nose of the ship and we swung round, using our main jets as additional brakes. Then he switched off the rotatory jets and there was a moment of terrifying confusion as the ship adjusted itself for a tail-landing.

With the jets thundering in my ears I watched the altimeter. *Nine hundred feet . . . seven hundred . . . five hundred. . . .*

"Jets off, Spike!"

The roaring died away, leaving no sound but a faint whistle of wind outside. The needle of the altimeter moved down. *Three hundred feet . . . two hundred . . . one hundred. . . .*

"Hold fast, everyone!"

There was a jarring thud, and the ship shivered and swayed. Then everything was silent, and we knew that we were home.

Uncle Lachlan smiled to Asa. "You've landed on Earth," he said. "The first person from another world ever to do so. I hope you won't be disappointed."

Spike came across from the control-panel. "I bet she won't! Wait till Madge gets cracking and she tastes her first ham and eggs!"

He pressed a button to open the main hatch. At the time I couldn't help thinking about Hermanoff, so far away on the lost planet, and I knew that my uncle and Professor Bergman were thinking about him, too.

Janet said: "Asa, you look out first."

She went across to the opening. "Why, it's beautiful!" she cried. "The dark green trees, and the river in the valley, and the house beyond. And look

—our little white flower that you call Charity—it is growing in your garden."

"Yes, my dear," said Professor Bergman. "We planted it there the first time we came back from Hesikos. It is spreading—slowly but surely."

Uncle Lachlan put his arm about my shoulders. "Who knows?" he said, quietly. "Perhaps while Asa is here it will spread more quickly."